"Hope."

One look and her body froze. Right there in the beating sun, she couldn't even feel her heartbeat.

Joel Kidd, the boyfriend who'd walked out on her eighteen months ago, stood next to the helicopter.

Black T-shirt, olive cargo pants and sunglasses to hide those dark eyes. From this distance she could see the ever-present dark scruff around his chin. His black hair was longer, grown out from the short military style she remembered.

She could see the gun strapped to his hip and knew Joel knew how to use it. That used to scare her a little. Now it comforted her frazzled nerves.

"What are you doing here?" The whip of her voice mirrored her frustration.

He hesitated, as if weighing what to say and whether to let his question go. Whatever he saw in her expression had him closing the distance between them. "I came to find you."

LAWLESS

—

HelenKay Dimon

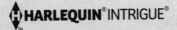

To my husband for agreeing to watch all those big budget Hollywood action movies with me and pretending I was telling the truth when I called them writing research

ISBN-13: 978-0-373-74814-3

LAWLESS

Copyright © 2014 by HelenKay Dimon

Printed in U.S.A.

ABOUT THE AUTHOR

Award-winning author HelenKay Dimon spent twelve years in the most unromantic career ever—divorce lawyer. After dedicating all that effort to helping people terminate relationships, she is thrilled to deal in happy endings and write romance novels for a living. Now her days are filled with gardening, writing, reading and spending time with her family in and around San Diego. HelenKay loves hearing from readers, so stop by her website, www.helenkaydimon.com, and say hello.

Books by HelenKay Dimon

CAST OF CHARACTERS

Joel Kidd—The former DIA agent endured a rough upbringing with a survivalist father. Joel turned to a life in intelligence work and landed a coveted position with the Corcoran Team, but he walked away from the one woman who meant everything to him. When he gets word she needs help, he comes running. Question is if he'll have the strength to leave her again.

Hope Algier—Hope knows about roughing it. She loves being in the sunshine and thrives on a challenge. She's conquered climbing and archery, and now she's leading outdoor adventures for business executives in need of a little team building. One of the men in her group goes missing in the middle of the West Virginia backcountry, but nothing prepares her for the arrival of Joel—the man she loves but wants to hate.

Tony Prather—The sharp businessman takes struggling companies and turns them around. This time he plans to make a home and be not only the savior of Baxter Industries but its new CEO. First he has to explain some missing money and odd sales figures. Maybe sending his executive staff on a retreat will make the trouble go away.

Mark Callah—Baxter's vice president of finance has a bit of an ego problem. When he goes missing on the business retreat after waving a gun around, no one suspects Hope, but they do wonder if he's a victim or the one firing the shots in the forest.

Jeff Acheson—The blowhard businessman thinks he knows everything. He's also hiding a company secret under all that ego. But when the bullets start flying, which side will he take?

Lance Ringer—He is the lowest ranking executive on the retreat. He also appears to be rock-solid. He's a new dad and the one who stays calm when everything goes wrong. Then again, looks can be deceiving....

Charlie Bardon—As the owner and chef at the camp where the business retreat is being held, he's right in the center of it all. He tries to get the businessmen to safety. He has weapons and skills. He can be a great asset to Hope and Joel...but can they trust him?

Connor Bowen—The leader of the Corcoran Team is wrestling with some heavy-duty secrets of his own, but when his men need him, he appears. He's focused and determined, but everyone wants to know the same thing—where is his wife?

Chapter One

Hope Algier preferred sunshine and fresh air to a stuffy office. Except today.

She spent most of her life outdoors. Her father had tried for years to entice his baby girl into the boardroom of the family business with promises of expensive cars and impressive bonus packages. She turned them all down without a second thought, but right now a leather chair behind a big desk sounded good.

Trees towered over her and surrounded her on every side. This section of land adjacent to West Virginia's Cranberry Wilderness was called the Cranberry Backcountry for a reason. It consisted of more than eleven thousand acres of hills and woods and little else.

Animals skittered around her. Leaves rustled as the summer wind blew warm air under her ponytail and across the back of her neck. Thick branches blocked most of the sunlight, giving her an eerie sense of isolation.

No people, no houses and no easy way out.

Turned out, this patch of forest messed with her satellite phone. She needed open sky for a signal, and she could only see peeks of blue through the canopy of summer green leaves above her. Right about now she'd give anything for a second of heat on her face.

She slipped behind a large trunk and leaned against it. Her heartbeat hammered in her ears as she slipped the sat phone out of the pocket of her cargo shorts. It measured a bit longer than a cell phone and fit in her palm. The map she'd memorized earlier and carried in her back pocket pointed to a clearing up ahead. She hoped she was close enough to catch a signal.

Please let it work this time.

She pushed buttons. When that didn't do anything, she smacked the side, hoping to jolt it into action. She even thought about smashing it against the cushion of dirt and leaves under her hiking boots.

She was about to repeat the hitting cycle when something crunched off to her right…again. The same subtle crackling she'd been hearing on and off since she'd dove deep into the trees. A squirrel, probably. She repeated the comment in her head over and over, hoping to reassure her brain and stop the sudden subtle shake moving through her hands. She refused to think bear or, worse, predator of the two-legged kind.

As she shifted, the stray branches scratched her bare legs and caught on the short sleeve of her cotton tee. She balanced her head against the hard bark again and counted to five. It took all of her control not to call out for Mark Callah, the vice president of finance for Baxter Industries.

He'd been all gung ho about "roughing it" on this corporate retreat. So much so he had brought a gun along without telling her. She saw it when he had waved it around last night at dinner. As the person leading the retreat, she had confiscated it. That didn't go over well. Now he was missing.

Crack.

There it was again. That made the fourth time she picked up the sound she wanted to write off as nothing. Something furry and four-legged and small…she hoped. But the gentle thuds sped up.

She peeked around the tree she was using as a shield and spied what looked like a flash of blue in the distance. The same flash she'd seen twice so far on this journey to find Mark and grab a clear shot to the satellite to jumpstart the phone.

She'd left the rest of the executives back at camp with orders to make breakfast and clean up. Except for Mark, they weren't exactly the venture-out-alone types. She strained to remember any of them wearing navy this morning at roll call, but her brain refused to focus.

Crunching and snapping echoed all around her until she couldn't tell from which direction the noises originated. The tunnel effect had her doubting her hearing and her vision. If she spun around one more time or ventured too far in any direction, she'd need the GPS to guide her back to camp.

What she really wanted was a view of open sky. If she could get to the edge of the field and send out a call for help, then she could duck back into the woods again.

Maybe she could lure out her visitor. Not that the option sounded too reassuring to her right now.

Without thinking, she reached for the leather sheath hooked to her belt. Her fingers skimmed over the hilt of her knife. She wanted to slide it out for protection, but running on uneven ground with a blade struck her as a distinctly stupid thing to do.

Still, having the makeshift weapon lessened the anxiety pounding through her. A little.

With one last glance into the thick columns of trees behind her, she took off. Her hands swatted at the branches blocking her forged path as her feet slipped over rocks and roots and her pace picked up to a jog. The wind whistled by her and the slap of leaves hit her face. She made enough noise to put a target on her back, but she didn't care. She needed that open field.

Footsteps fell hard off to her left this time. The thump of shoes against the ground kicked up and the person drew almost parallel to her position. She tried to zigzag even though she knew her white shirt would give her position away...wherever she was.

But she needed space and enough distance to make the call and pull her knife. Regardless of whatever or whoever else was out there, she would not go down without a fight.

The trail in front of her brightened and sunlight puddled on the forest floor. Even without the thinning of branches she knew she was close from the beep of her GPS as she zoned in on the preset location. The sat phone smacked against her leg with each step. She fumbled to pull it out of her pocket and hold it as she ran.

The log came out of nowhere. A fallen tree too thick to jump over right in her path. She tried to pivot and her ankle turned. One second she was on her feet and the next her knee cracked against the hard ground and something sharp dug into her palm.

She was down for only a few seconds but long enough for heavy breathing to pound in her lungs and float through the trees. The labored sound drowned out everything. The running near her seemed to stop. She feared that meant someone or something circled nearby ready to grab her.

Ignoring the pain thumping from her foot to her hip, she pushed up. With her hands on the log, she skirted the end and ran. Each punch of her right foot against the hard ground made her teeth rattle with the need to cry out.

But the bright light was right there. A few more feet and she'd be free. She dodged a massive tree trunk as the crashing of footsteps beside her picked up again. A blue blur raced close enough for her to make out a figure, but the heavy hoodie pulled down low made it impossible to identify who it was.

But the *who* didn't matter right now.

She broke into the clearing and reached into her pocket for the phone. Nothing. She patted her shorts and spun around in a circle as desperation swamped her. Fear rumbled through her until her knees buckled.

The log. The fall. The memory came rushing back. She must have dropped the stupid thing on the ground when she went down.

With her back against a tree, she scanned the forty feet of open field in front of her and the miles of woods beyond that. She tried to calm her breathing and slow her heart enough for her to concentrate.

The adrenaline kept pumping. She knew she should welcome it because it kept the pain at bay and her mind off the blood around her knee and throbbing in her hand, but she needed to focus.

The figure, whoever it was, stood still, right behind a tree about fifty feet away. She slipped her knife out again and tightened her grip over the handle, ignoring the fresh burst of throbbing from her injury. She opened her mouth to call out, to make the idiot face her instead of trying to terrify her in silence.

A strange thwapping drowned out her yell. She shielded her eyes with a hand and squinted up into the sun. Blue skies greeted her. She didn't see anything, but the noise grew louder.

Whop, whop, whop.

A helicopter broke into sight as it came in for a landing. She blinked twice, not trusting what she was seeing. Out here, in the middle of nowhere, it didn't make sense.

Her breath hiccupped as a new panic crashed over her. She could have walked into anything. Drug runners or criminals of any type. And if the pilot was a partner to her tracker, there was no way a knife would save her.

The helicopter hovered over the ground. The blades kicked up grass and leaves. When it finally touched down, she could make out two men, but the glass, and probably the waves of fear, distorted her view.

She was about to slip back into the blanket of the woods where she at least stood a chance when the rustling off to her left had her attention dragging back to the tree and the person hiding there. The hoodie was gone. Fearing the attacker could sneak up on her, she backed to the edge of the open field and held her knife in front of her as she faced the woods.

"Hope."

She thought she heard her name over the chopping of the helicopter blades, but she knew that wasn't possible. No way had one of her executives ventured away from the camp and somehow made it this far.

Her mind had gone into shutdown mode. That was the only explanation. She was hearing things and jumping at every sound.

The helicopter's engine wound down and the propeller slowed to a lazy turn. The change had her spinning around to face the new threat. One look and her body froze. Right there in the beating sun, every organ inside her whirred to a stop. She couldn't even feel her heartbeat.

"Hope, what are you doing?" Joel Kidd, the boyfriend who had walked out on her eighteen months ago rather than fight for a life with her, stood next to the helicopter.

Black tee, olive cargo pants, and sunglasses to hide those near-black eyes. From this distance she could see the ever-present dark scruff around his chin. His black hair was longer, grown out from the short military style she remembered. He might even have been thinner. And none of that explained what he was doing in West Virginia.

With one last look into the menacing woods behind her, she stepped forward. She could see the gun strapped to his hip and knew Joel was well trained in how to use it. That used to scare her a little. Now it comforted her frazzled nerves.

"You cut your leg." He ripped his sunglasses off, and concerned eyes traveled over her. "What's going on?"

Seeing him hit her like a kick to the stomach. She almost doubled over from the force of it. She'd loved him and mourned his leaving, then had spent some time pretending she hated him. As she looked at him now, old feelings of longing came rushing back. So did the urge to punch him.

"What are you doing here?" The whip of her voice mirrored her frustration.

He hesitated as if weighing what to say and whether to let the question go. Whatever he saw on her face or in her expression had him closing the distance between them. "I came to find you."

"Why?" Truth was, he devoted his life to gathering intelligence and protecting others. Right now she could use a bit of both.

The sound of the helicopter seemed to have scared off her tracker, and for that reason alone she was willing to hear Joel out. For a few seconds.

"You haven't been picking up your phone." His gaze did another bounce up and down her body, hesitating over her torn-up knee. "Where is it?"

Good question. "Lost."

His near-black eyes narrowed. "Really?"

"Long story."

"Any chance of hearing it right now?"

"First, you answer a question of mine." She glanced past Joel to the pilot. He jumped down and headed for them.

"Shoot," Joel said.

"There is no way you just happened to be out here, tooling around West Virginia, when you live in Annapolis. So, what's going on?"

The corner of his mouth lifted in a smile. "You know where I live now?"

No way was she walking into that discussion. "Let's stick to my question."

"Fine, it's not a coincidence." Joel's expression went blank. "Your father sent me."

Figured. "It's still your turn to explain, so keep talking."

She loved her dad, but his protective streak

stayed locked in hyperdrive. He ran a private security company, one Joel used to work for. All that danger made her dad a bit paranoid. Though, admittedly, in this instance that was a good thing.

"Your dad and Baxter Industries." Joel shifted his weight, putting his feet hip-distance apart. "Seems your dad wanted you to have backup out here. Combine that with the twitchiness of the Baxter Board about having a twenty-six-year-old woman, alone, guiding the male executives, and you get me."

"How very sexist of them."

"They clearly don't appreciate how competent you are outdoors."

She had no idea if that was a shot or a compliment, so she ignored it. "If the phone isn't working, how did you…oh, right. The GPS locator still functions."

"Yes."

"So, Dad tracked me down and sent you by helicopter."

Instead of answering, Joel motioned to the pilot. "This is Cameron Roth."

She wasn't in the mood for meeting people just now, but there was no reason to be rude. "Okay."

"We work together," Joel explained.

"At where exactly?" She'd tried to find out where Joel went when he left her dad's company. One night, bored and feeling lonely, she con-

ducted a search, hoping to locate him, and un-
covered nothing.

Her father finally let slip Joel lived in Annapolis, less than an hour away from her place in Virginia, the same place he used to live with her but
never bothered to visit now. Being ignored made
her stop checking in on the guy. If Joel didn't care
enough to make contact, she wouldn't either.

"Ma'am." The other man butted in with a nod
of welcome. "You can call me Roth or Cam."

The guy looked about the same age as Joel, a
few years older than her, and shared Joel's used-
to-be-in-the-military look. Broad shoulders with
muscles peeking out from under the edge of his
T-shirt. They both carried their bodies in a permanent battle stance, as if they could shoot or tackle
at any moment, if needed.

Joel had the Tall, Dark and Whoa-He's-Hot
thing down. That hadn't changed in their months
apart. Cam's lighter hair and blue eyes made him
seem less intense, but knowing the male type
standing in front of her, she doubted that was actually the case.

Joel clapped. "There. That's settled."

Looked like the menfolk thought explanation
time was over. She disagreed. "Let's go back to
my question. Why are you really here? And skip
the sat phone talk this time."

"Your father sent me to look for you." That smile widened. "Now it's my turn to ask a question."

"Did you really answer mine?"

Cam laughed. "She has you there, man."

Joel nodded in the direction of her hand. "Is there a reason you're carrying a knife, or is the plan to stab the helicopter?"

She glanced down, then back at Joel. "Are you worried it's meant for you?"

"I take it you two know each other pretty well," Cam said.

The conversation kept jumping around. She'd only remembered the knife when Joel mentioned it. The burning from where it pressed into her palm suddenly hit her.

Then Cam's comment grabbed her attention.

"Joel didn't tell you who I was to him?" She wanted not to care, but the hurt swallowed up her indifference.

Cam looked from her to Joel and back again. "Let's just say I'm thinking he left out some important pieces about your joint past."

"Hope." Joel snapped his fingers and brought the focus back to him. "The knife?"

She stared at it in her hands. "What about it?"

"Why are you holding it as if you're ready to attack?"

She couldn't come up with a reason to stall and

certainly had no reason to lie. Not about this. Not to him. "Someone was following me."

Both men leaned in closer, all amusement gone from their faces. Cam's mouth opened, but Joel was the one who barked out a question. "What?"

Now that she had their attention, she decided to spill it all. "And I think one of my executives might be dead."

Chapter Two

Joel called up every ounce of his practiced control to stay calm. Before he'd joined the Corcoran Team, a private security organization out of Annapolis, Maryland, that specialized in risk assessments for companies and governments, this sort of thing would have had him spinning and drilling her with questions.

Connor Bowen and the rest of the Corcoran Team had taught him the importance of patience and holding still for the right opening. Without those skills, the high-priority, under-the-radar kidnap and rescue missions they conducted would fail. Because when you worked outside the legal parameters and without a safety net, mistakes couldn't happen.

After a lifetime of kicking around in the intelligence field, Joel knew he'd finally landed in a place that felt right. He'd buckled down, used his tech skills to fill in after the last tech guy left and tried to forget about her. Hope, his greatest weakness.

Now he seriously considered telling Cam to get lost for a few minutes, though he doubted the guy would budge. Not when he was staring as if he'd never seen a woman before and was hanging on every word of the discussion.

Joel couldn't really blame Cam on the gawking part. Hope looked as good as Joel remembered. Better, even. The long dark brown hair and near black eyes hadn't changed. From the dimple and girl-next-door hotness to the tanned legs and smokin' petite frame, he found her almost impossible to resist.

Add in her smarts, competency with weapons and near fearless determination when she wanted something and he'd had no choice but to dump his job and move to the next state to keep from falling deeper into her. Or that's what he'd rationalized at the time.

But right now he worried more about the danger that appeared to be haunting her. "Say that again."

She cleared her throat. "I have a missing executive."

Joel had no idea what that meant. "You said dead a second ago."

She shrugged. "I'm hoping that was an exaggeration."

Well, that cleared up…nothing. He glanced over at Cam.

He shook his head. "Got me. I have no clue."

"Hope." Joel reached out to touch the hand with the weapon in it and felt the subtle tremor running through her. Yeah, forget how comfortable she looked hanging around outside, something bad had happened and she was throwing off the desperation vibe.

His protective instincts kicked into high gear. He folded his hand over hers and slid the knife out of her palm. Not an easy task since she had a death grip on it.

Moving nice and slow, he eased the blade back into its case at her waist as he rubbed his thumb over the deep creases on her palm. "Where is this executive?"

"His name is Mark Callah."

"Okay." Joel didn't dig too deep for details. Not yet. "Where is Mark?"

"I have no idea since I lost him."

Cam grunted. "She's giving you a pretty logical answer, actually."

"I got up this morning and he was gone from camp." She tugged free of Joel's hold and rubbed her hands together. "I headed for this clearing to use the sat phone and realized some guy was following me. Then your helicopter—"

"Hold up." For the second time, she jumped right past the most interesting part. "Go back a second."

"To where?"

Stray branches crunched under Cam's feet as he shifted his weight. "I'm guessing to the 'following me' part."

She spent a second frowning at both of them. "Blue hoodie. The guy stalked me, then started moving faster and came up the side until we were parallel. He didn't look up and stayed close. Your helicopter scared him off."

"Stalked?" Joel didn't hear much after that word.

"Yes, Joel." She didn't roll her eyes, but she looked like she was right on the edge of doing so.

She could sigh at him all she wanted because he was not letting this conversation drop. Not until he assessed the level of danger. "Could this person be one of the executives you have out here on the team-building retreat?"

This time her face went blank. "Wow, my dad really did fill you in on this job."

"Let's stick to your story for now." One more diversion and Joel worried he'd never be able to pull the tale out of her. And he knew from experience any talk about her dad and his protective nature would not make this exercise go faster.

"Except for Mark, most of the Baxter Industries management talk tough but are terrified of being out here. One guy jumped around demanding to go home because he found a tick on his upper arm." She snorted. "I mean, come on."

Joel bit back a laugh. "Very manly."

"Right. So, you understand why I can't imagine any of them chasing me through the woods, being covert and ducking out of sight for no good reason."

"You're throwing out some scary words there."

"So?"

She could shoot and run and build a camp from twigs, but that didn't make her invincible. He wondered if she understood that. "My point is this story gets worse the more details you add."

She glanced over her shoulder and deep into the woods behind her. "Anyway, I'd like to think if it was one of my guys, he would have helped or at least called out when I fell."

The bad news just kept coming. Joel glanced at Cam. "And now we have a fall."

She faced them again. "What?"

"You skipped that part before," Cam said.

Joel guessed that was intentional. "Let's just say your linear storytelling needs work."

"I'll run through all of it if you need me to—"

"I do." Joel wanted her comment to stop right there.

She talked right over his interruption. "But since you're here, you can come with me while I get my sat phone and then we can spread out and hunt for Mark."

Joel caught her in the second before she took

off. Never mind her tale about a stalker and the terror in her eyes only a few minutes ago. Now she was ready to head out. "I thought you lost the phone."

"Yeah, but I know where."

"Your definition of lost is no better than your storytelling ability."

"We don't have time for chitchat." Her gaze dipped to where his fingers wrapped around her elbow, then bounced back up again. "I'm assuming you guys need to get out of here and head off to some other covert action-movie adventure, so let's move."

Nice try. "You're my job this week, remember?"

"Yeah, we're going to talk about that later."

"Talk all you want. I'm staying." That had been the plan before the knife and the story about the fall and every other bizarre fact she threw out, and he wasn't changing it now.

But there was some good news here. Her feistiness clicked back into place with full force. While the verbal jabs about his job used to drive him nuts, he missed this side of her, too.

She didn't back down. She didn't care about his size or ability with a weapon. She understood he'd never hurt her and held her ground. Probably had something to do with having a former special ops father who made sure his precious daughter and only child could protect herself no matter what.

The attitude had gotten her in trouble more than once. Not with him, but some of the men in her father's business, Algier Security, didn't appreciate her refusal to be a good little girl and sit down.

Sexist idiots.

Still, she could be rough on the male ego. He glanced over at Cam to fill him in with a simple explanation. "She doesn't approve of what we do."

"Understood," Cam said with a nod.

Hope wasn't having any of it. She shot them both one of her men-can-be-clueless frowns. "That's not true."

Cam kept nodding, as if he'd figured out some great big secret. "Is that why you left him?"

Damn. "Let's not go there." This was just about the last topic Joel wanted to discuss.

Strike that. It was *the* last. Dead last.

"I figured it out." Cam smiled. "She's the ex."

Suddenly Joel regretted that one night a month or so ago with too much beer and too much talking. Cam had wanted to know why Joel never dated and he mentioned a tough break-up. Cam clearly put it all together.

"Didn't he tell you the story?" Hope's eyebrow lifted. "Interesting."

"How so?" Cam asked.

"Joel left me."

Cam's eyes bugged as his jaw dropped. "No way."

"I know, right?" She shook her head. "Whatever."

Cam whistled. "I didn't see that news coming."

That was enough of that. Joel cleared his throat to get everyone's attention. "Can we get back to the missing guy and the stalking?"

"Camp is back here." She didn't wait for a discussion or arguments. She headed off through the thick branches, with twigs and other debris crunching under her boots. She slowed down only long enough to glance over her shoulder and gesture for them to follow.

"Hope…and she's gone." Joel took a step in the same direction.

Cam slid in and blocked his path. "You dumped her?"

"Let it go."

Cam laughed. "I think we both know that's not going to happen."

It was a long story and Joel knew he didn't exactly come off well. With his messed-up upbringing, a quiet life in the suburbs wasn't on the table. But she had tempted him, made him think even for a little while that he could do normal. Then he got offered a dream job with the Defense Intelligence Agency and, like an idiot, picked it over her.

Funny how karma nailed him on that one.

Cam leaned in with a hand behind his ear. "Not talking?"

"Nope."

"You will." He winked, then called out to Hope. "Hey, where was this stalker walking?"

She stopped and gestured to the line of trees directly across from her. "About fifty feet that way, running parallel with me."

Joel tracked her white shirt as she pushed long branches out of her way and kept walking. "Notice how she acts like whatever happened wasn't a big deal."

"Was she ever an operative?"

"Mountain climber, archery expert, like Olympic skill level, outdoors type and can shoot better than some members of the Corcoran Team."

"You're talking about Ben, right?" Cam asked.

Ben Tanner was the newest member of the Corcoran Team and a former special agent for NCIS. The guy could shoot but he lacked the sniper skills of many on the team. And they never let him forget it. "Obviously."

Cam stopped staring at Hope, and it looked like that took some control on his part. "Explain to me why you left her again? Because, gotta be honest, man, between the way she looks, the way she moves and that list of skills you just read off, I think I'm in love."

"Get over it."

Cam nodded, which he often did. "Ah, okay. Interesting."

Hope's white shirt got farther away. That meant

one thing—the time for talk had ended. "Stop with that crap."

Just as Joel lost sight of her, she peeked out from behind a massive tree trunk. "You guys coming?"

This time Cam laughed. "Your ex wants your attention."

"Don't call her that." Correct or not, the term grated on Joel's nerves. It meant she was free to find someone else, and even though he knew that was fair and the right thing, he despised the idea.

He'd spent the months away from her pretending he didn't care when her father had called to alert him that she'd gone out on a date with this guy or that one. The old man was on a warped matchmaking mission. One that slowly broke Joel until he thought he'd go insane imagining her in bed with someone else.

"I am so happy I was available to fly you in for this op. Wouldn't have missed this for anything." Cam clapped Joel on the back. "Not sure who will enjoy this more—the guys back at the Annapolis office or the guys on my traveling team. Tough call."

Both options sucked for Joel. "I could hide your body out here."

"You're welcome to try."

Because Cam came to Corcoran with the nickname "Lethal" and rumor was he'd flown Navy missions so secret just mentioning the operation names would bring the FBI running with guns firing, Joel decided to switch the subject. "And this is a favor for an old friend, not an op."

"If a businessman is missing and someone is chasing your woman, it's an op." Cam didn't wait around for an argument. He headed in the direction Hope indicated as the stalker's path. "I'll be over there, straining to hear every word."

Joel took off after Hope. She'd stopped, and with his long stride, he caught up fast. When he drew close he saw her standing near a fallen tree, staring at the dirt.

"What's going on?" he asked.

She looked up, the anger obvious in her tight jaw and the flush of red on her cheeks. "My phone is gone."

"I thought we already knew that."

"No, I mean I had it in my hand while I was running—"

"You ran through this?"

"—and stumbled here. I dropped the phone and now it's gone."

There was no trail and no obvious signs of a path. Roots poked out of the ground, and the trees had grown to the point where they blanketed the area. Any sane person would watch her step. But she had run. Figured.

He thought about lecturing her but abandoned

the idea when she bent down and started patting the rough terrain with her palm. Hope knew the outdoors, loved and cherished the openness. It was one of the things they had in common.

Still, a phone could only bounce so far. "Any chance you lost it somewhere else?"

"No." She tried to reach her arm under the log. "I'm not exactly easy to spook. I know what I'm talking about."

"But you are."

She tugged on her arm but didn't remove it or sit back up again. Twisting around, she looked up at him. "What?"

"Spooked." And stuck. He wondered how long it would be before she admitted that. "Your pulse is racing and you're jumpy. Not that long ago you were shaking and holding that knife like you were ready to slash anyone in your path."

"Someone was chasing me." She kept shifting and squirming. The heels of her boots dug into the dirt as she wrenched her shoulder.

Much more of this and she'd really injure herself. Any second now she'd ask for help. Well, most people would. With Hope, who knew?

He was ready to jump in. She just had to say the word, but he'd bet all the cash on him she wouldn't.

"I get the chasing part," he said.

She stopped moving around and shot him a big-eyed stare. "You don't believe me."

With Hope, he figured that was as close as he was going to get to a plea for help. He crouched and did the quick math on the best angle to pull her out without dislocating her shoulder. "I didn't say that."

"I am not a little girl who needs protecting. Your days of holding that job are over and, in case you missed it, I was never a little girl on your watch."

"Oh, I noticed." He jammed his fingers into the hard ground as dirt and peat moss slid under his nails. Ignoring the closeness and the way her arm brushed across his chest, he wedged his hand under hers and dug a shallow tunnel with his knuckles. "For the record, I noticed everything about you. Still do."

Before he could add to the comment, footsteps echoed around him and boots appeared in front of his face. He strained to look up and got as far as the familiar utility pants.

"Our company is back," Joel said into the relative quiet of the forest.

She tried to spin around and hissed when her trapped arm stopped her movements. It took another beat for her to get a word out. "Where?"

"He means me." Cam dropped down to the balls

of his feet with his body between Joel and Hope. "What are you two doing?"

With his hand caked with dirt, Joel wrapped his fingers around her bare arm and gave a quick pull. "Rescuing her."

"I don't need rescuing." She popped free and fell back on her butt. Next she rubbed her shoulder joint. "Ouch."

Joel refused to feel guilty for getting her unstuck when she'd been too stubborn to ask for his assistance. "Good thing you weren't caught then."

"Glad we cleared that up." Cam stood. "She's right about being followed. There are footprints over there."

"Any clue about who or why?" Joel got to his feet and put a hand down, surprised when she took it to jump up next to him.

"Some interesting information." Cam turned his camera around and flashed an image most people would think showed nothing but leaves but really showed an outline of a shoe. "Men's size eleven. Probably a hundred-seventy pounds."

She leaned in closer to the screen, her eyes narrowing. "You can tell that from a grainy picture?"

Cam nodded. "And your stalker is an overpronator."

Joel had to smile at that. "Now you're just showing off."

Cam shrugged. "I'm good at my job."

"Which is what again?" she asked.

No way was Joel entertaining an impromptu debriefing in the middle of an isolated forest. Protocol was very clear. The Corcoran Team operated on a need-to-know basis.

To the world they provided risk assessments and moved in to help if things went wrong. Important but not the complete story. The definition missed the reality of the constant danger and huge amount of shooting.

Fact was, telling the woman he once dated about his current occupation had to violate some rule. "Not up for discussion."

She sighed. "I've been hearing that my whole life."

A stark silence followed her words. Joel didn't bother to explain the real-world need for not filling her in. She knew how this game was played. She'd lived with a man known for having secrets. Joel got that she hated the game, but that didn't change it one bit.

Cam finally broke the quiet with a clap that thundered through the trees. "So, we have someone skulking around the woods."

"And a missing phone." She turned on Joel with a finger in his face. "Do not ask me if I'm sure this is where I dropped it."

Those words died in his throat because saying them could get him punched. "No, ma'am."

She treated him to a smile then. "That's new."

He tried not to notice how it lit up her face. "I'm not always difficult."

"Yes, you are," she said.

Cam nodded at the same time. "Not always, but mostly."

"We should head back and make sure none of these weekend warriors cut off a toe." Falling back into command mode kept Joel from telling both of them off. "We also need to check out Hope's knee."

She glanced down.

Cam nodded. "Maybe this Mark guy wandered into camp and there's some reasonable explanation for all of this."

The men started to walk but she stayed still. "What about your helicopter and wherever you were planning to go after stopping in here?"

Sounded like she still wasn't understanding his assignment here. Joel tried again. "This is my final destination. With you."

Cam slid his foot over the piles of leaves stacked around them. "And I'm good to hang out for a few hours."

Her hands went to her hips, and her legs still didn't move. "You both think something is seriously wrong."

Joel decided not to sugarcoat this. Sure, the past half hour could mean nothing. Or it could mean

Baxter Industries and her dad were right to send in reinforcements. They wouldn't know until they got back to camp. "Stolen phone and a stalker? Yeah, Hope. Something is not right."

Her smile came roaring back. "Good."

He wondered if he would ever understand her mood swings. "How is that good?"

"Because you believe me. You're not writing this off as some hysterical woman thing."

Of all the things she could have said, that one came out of nowhere. "I've never known you to be hysterical."

She eyed him up. "You know, you seem slightly smarter about women now. Maybe some things have changed about you since we last went out."

And he worried the most obvious—how much he wanted her—hadn't.

Chapter Three

Hope tried to ignore Joel for the entire walk back to camp. His constant stream of questions didn't make that easy. He wanted to know about the campers and what her plan had been to get the men in and out of camp. She gave the details, even though she really wanted to stop and demand an explanation for why it was so easy for him to walk out of her life.

Then again, maybe she didn't want to know. Her ego could only take so much, and he had the power to break her. Had from the minute she'd met him.

The forest floor crunched and crackled under their feet. Their steps echoed around her, and Cam whistled as he walked a half step behind her. It all seemed so normal…except for the missing businessman and lost phone. And who could forget the scary stalker?

Amazing how a nice morning could make a left turn into awful so quickly.

She had taken this job to emotionally recuperate. The double whammy of losing Joel and the disaster on her last climbing expedition had sent her world into a tailspin. A new career conducting business retreats and leading simple hiking and camping outings was supposed to be soothing. The way her nerves jumped around was anything but.

"Looks like we're here."

The sound of Cam's voice over her shoulder made her jump and knock into Joel next to her. When her hands brushed against his, a new sensation spun through her. Something like excitement, and that didn't make her happy at all. She wanted to be totally over him, or at the very least not feel anything. She'd do anything for a bit of indifference at the moment.

She settled for doubling her pace and broke through the trees and into the camp clearing a step before her self-appointed bodyguards. The businessmen sat on logs turned into benches around the fire pit area. They looked up as she approached.

They all started talking a second later. Shouting over each other in an attempt to hold the metaphorical floor.

Yeah, she hadn't missed this part of their company dynamic during the past hour.

"Where have you been?" Jeff Acheson, the

Baxter director of marketing, dumped his plate on the ground and stood up. His distaste for her was on full display, from his puffing red cheeks to the scowl marring what she guessed most women found to be his perfectly chiseled model face.

She took a long look at him in the bright sunshine and decided he was a bit too buffed and polished for her taste. He had a phony air about him. Probably because he listed his age as thirty-four on the questionnaire she had handed out last night to assess their skill levels, when she knew from the files Baxter gave her the number was more like forty.

That sort of thing struck her as ridiculous. She'd bet he took twice as long to get ready for a big date than she did.

She could still remember the up-and-down sweep he gave her when they'd first met in the Baxter offices. He'd turned on the charming smile back when he thought she was some sort of assistant to the *real* leader on the trip. That disappeared when she'd made it clear she was in charge.

But he picked the wrong time to get all uppity with her. She wasn't in the mood. "Is Mark here?"

"What?" Lance Ringer, the Baxter personnel manager, asked.

Lance was the one guy Hope had liked immediately. He was the youngest on the retreat but didn't try to impress her. He owned up to the fact he hadn't been camping since he was a kid, more than twenty years ago, and would rather be home with his newborn and wife than out roughing it with the guys. Hope found his honesty refreshing.

"Mark was missing this morning and I went to look for him," she said, waiting for Joel and Cam to pipe up and feeling a bit dazed when neither rushed to take the lead. "Did he ever come back?"

Jeff took a threatening step in her direction. "Why didn't you tell us there was a problem before now?"

"Probably because of this type of overblown reaction." Joel morphed from calm to a shield of muscles in two seconds. He reached around Hope, blocking some of her view of Jeff, and put a hand on his chest. "Back up."

Jeff tried to push Joel's hand away. "Who are you?"

"Not relevant at the moment."

Joel didn't move and Cam just smiled. Hope was smart enough to know those reactions meant brewing trouble. Joel's protective nature made it tough for him to back down, and when he was faced with a pontificating blowhard like Jeff, there was no telling what could happen.

"You have a gun," Jeff said.

Joel motioned toward Cam. "We both do."

With the tension building and washing over all

of them, she decided this might be a good time to make one point clear. "Joel is my assistant."

She put her hand over his and it dropped away from Jeff. But the battle stance stayed, as did Joel's unwavering gaze on Jeff.

Cam covered his smile with his hand as he mumbled, "This should be good."

"What are you talking about?" Jeff asked as he turned his attention back to her. "I thought you were the supposed leader of this outing."

She said the word *assistant* and Jeff assumed she was no longer in charge. The man heard what he wanted to hear.

Before anyone said anything else that made her grumbly, Hope made the necessary introductions to keep the chain of command clear. "This is Joel Kidd, my helper, and Cameron Roth."

Joel cleared his throat. "Helper?"

With a raise of the chin she held her ground. "Yes."

The silence lasted for only a second before he nodded. "Alrighty then."

Relief poured through her when he didn't push it. She turned back to Lance. "Where's Perry?"

"Who's that?" Cam asked.

Lance got up and brushed off his pants. He stopped to shake hands with everyone. "Perry Kramer is our sales manager."

"What does he sell?" Joel stared at Hope when

she shoved an elbow into his stomach. "What? It's a fair question."

Lance shrugged. "But it's probably not important information right now."

Hope heard the rustle of branches and glanced over in time to see Charlie Bardon, the camp owner and cook, break through the trees on the far side of the last cabin. He was out of breath and running his hands over his grimy chef's apron as he walked.

"What's going on out here?" he asked.

Joel looked to the newcomer. "That was going to be my question."

Charlie didn't look any more willing to back down than Joel. They stood face to face and shared the same former military in-command presence. Pushing fifty, Charlie had been out for decades, but Joel seemed just as determined and set in his ways at thirty-three.

Before this could blow into a full-blown argument, Hope tried to step in. "Mark is missing."

"I was hoping he was with you." Charlie turned his attention to Joel. "Where did you come from?"

Joel shrugged. "Annapolis…or are you looking for an explanation about how birthing works?"

The older man's eyes narrowed. "Are you trying to be funny?"

"Not really."

"Okay, enough." She wasn't sure who deserved

the bigger kick to the shin—Joel for acting disinterested and maintaining his monotone voice through the snide comments or Cam, who couldn't stop smiling. "Cam and Joel came in by helicopter to help me."

If possible, Charlie's scowl deepened. "With what?"

She had no idea how to answer the question, so she skipped it and talked to the campers, trying to ignore the fact another one appeared to be missing. "When is the last time anyone saw Mark?"

Taking a long time and making the movement last longer than necessary, Jeff folded his arms in front of him. "When you two fought last night."

Joel turned to face her. "Really?"

"He stormed out, saying he was going to the cabin," Lance said. "But he wasn't in there when I went to bed."

"What time was that?" Cam asked.

"Around midnight."

Charlie blew out a long breath as he talked. "You didn't think that was odd?"

"He was ticked off that Hope took his gun. I thought I heard him coming in later, but he wasn't there this morning." Lance looked at Joel as if he expected backup.

Joel leaned in closer instead. "His what?"

She knew there was no way that comment would slide by. "Gun, and I'll explain later."

"Yeah, you will," Joel said.

But not now. Not when all those eyes focused solely on her. "Go on, Lance."

"That's it. I figured he was walking it off or getting something to eat. Honestly, I didn't think it was a big deal. He got scolded. Get over it."

Hope didn't know what to do with any of that information. Mark had gotten angry and stormed off. She knew that before she took off on her search. But maybe she could get an answer to one question. "Were either of you out in the woods this morning?"

She got a lot of head shaking and mumbling but no answers. She scanned the crowd. Only Lance didn't possess the right body type. He'd joked about gaining more weight than his wife during the pregnancy. Hope doubted that was true, but he was carrying around a few extra pounds that would have made it a bit tough to dodge in and out of the trees.

Still, that didn't mean none of them had done it. Someone had and the nerves jumping around inside her wouldn't quiet down until she had answers, the right number of campers and her phone.

"And where were you this morning?" Joel asked the man in front of him.

Charlie didn't move. "Checking on the food situation."

From the question Hope guessed Joel wasn't

as willing to believe as easily as she was. Then again, he'd just met the group, and they were down two members.

"Let's try it this way." Joel shifted his weight. Not a big move. Barely perceptible but something about it made him appear taller and less willing to play games. "When did you last see Mark?"

Charlie's gaze bounced from Joel to Cam and back again. "What's with the weapons? Are you police?"

The look on Joel's face, the way the corner of his mouth inched up, came close to a smile. "Pretend I am."

Charlie didn't share his amusement. "I don't think I will."

Much more of this and they'd never get to an answer. As it was, Lance and Jeff stared, watching the verbal volleys with their mouths hanging more open with each sentence.

Hope decided to act like what she was—in charge. "Charlie, help me out here. Mark wandered off and now I don't know where Perry is."

"I'm pretty sure Perry is in taking a second run at the chow line."

This time the relief walloped the air right out of her lungs. "So, you've seen him this morning?"

Charlie nodded. "About fifteen minutes ago."

"That's a relief," Lance said.

She saw Joel opening his mouth to say something and jumped in first. "But it doesn't explain the Mark issue."

Charlie waved her off. Even threw in a "bah" right before he started talking. "He's just blowing off steam."

The men kept saying it, but the explanation wasn't good enough. "I can't find him and I need him to check in before we do one more thing."

Jeff swiped his thermos off the ground. "We need to go out looking for him."

"How exactly?" Joel asked.

The question caused Jeff to go still. "What?"

Hope knew where this was going. She felt the conversation rolling downhill and couldn't grab a two-second break to throw her body in front of it.

She couldn't speak for Cam's expertise, but she guessed it was off the charts. But Joel knew everything about surviving outdoors. He was the one person in the group better at outdoor activities than she was, and that was saying something.

He thrived in this environment. His father had groomed his kids to fight and shoot, readying them for the domestic civil war he insisted was coming.

Lost in paranoia and reeling from the unexpected loss of his wife, Joel's dad believed the government had lost its way and only small pockets of freedom-loving people would save the world. He went about it by toughening up his kids, making them sleep outside and denying them an education until the state stepped in.

The upbringing was sick and wrong and it shaped Joel in ways she still hadn't explored. He liked to joke and act as if certain things didn't bother him, but she knew. But there were times when his gaze would wander and those dark eyes would glaze. He'd go to whatever place he built in his mind to find normalcy. And he wouldn't let her in.

"Do you know anything about wilderness survival?" His voice stayed deceptively soft as he aimed the question at Jeff.

The other man held eye contact for a few seconds, then broke it. "We studied up before we came out here."

"Oh, good." Joel stared at Cam. "They studied."

She got the point, but the conversation promised to run them right into a brick wall. "Joel, that's enough."

Not that he heard her. He continued to stare at Jeff.

She knew the hard truth. None of the testosterone-jousting did anything to help them locate Mark.

"Which cabin belongs to this guy?" Cam asked.

"That one." She pointed to the building directly next to where hers sat in the middle of the makeshift line. Because she appreciated the assist, she followed Cam's lead. "Charlie, can you take the guys and put together some provisions? If we're going to spread out and search for Mark—"

Joel frowned. "Are we?"

"—they need to be ready."

Charlie started shaking his head before she finished the sentence. "I'm not convinced this is necessary. He's probably sulking. Struck me as the type."

"He's the vice president of finance," Jeff said, as if that explained everything.

When Joel finally performed that eye roll it looked like he'd been dying to do since Jeff stood up, it was obvious he wasn't convinced. "So?"

But she had a plan and it depended on everyone agreeing and moving on. "Charlie, if you could, maybe, keep everyone together, that would be a great help."

He stared at her, not saying a thing. A gust of wind shook the leaves and the sun beat down on the campground, but the silence stretched out. Finally, Charlie began a slow nod. It picked up in speed as it went and seemed to last for a long time. "Ah, got it."

She blew out the breath she'd been holding. It scratched her throat as it rushed out. "Thanks."

"Gentlemen?" Charlie motioned for the managers to follow him. "Let's go find Perry and get packed."

Joel didn't speak until the place cleared out

and the voices faded as everyone slipped through the path between the cabins and headed for the kitchen cabin and open seating area about thirty feet away before he faced her. "What's with the search party talk?"

"Some of this crew think they are mountain men. I was worried they'd run off with butter knives and try to slay bears or something equally stupid." She'd dealt with the type for a long time and developed some skills, the top one being not to let them rally and slide into attack mode.

Cam nodded. "You wanted Charlie to keep them occupied while we searched."

She looked at Joel, waited for him to say something. She expected a lecture on knowing the parameters of her job and leaving the investigation to him, the professional.

Instead a smile broke across his lips. "Your dad would be proud of your covert abilities."

The compliment rushed right to her head, making her as dizzy as drinking the finest wine. "You don't grow up with a former special ops guy and not learn a few things."

That smile only widened. "Apparently."

"Besides, Charlie gets it. He knows the kind of people who come out here," she said, hoping to focus on all she had to do and drag her mind away from Joel. "He can help."

Cam chuckled. "If Joel doesn't tick him off."

Very true. "Well, there's that."

They walked to Mark's cabin. The men's footsteps matched and she had to push her gait to keep up. They had long legs and moved quickly and quietly. She had a case of nerves that shook her hard enough to knock her over. She wanted to believe there was a reasonable explanation, but as the minutes passed her faith waned.

She used her master key to open the lock. All three of them stepped inside and stopped. Their shoulders touched and they still took up most of the open space.

They kept silent as their gazes scanned from wall to wall. The room consisted of two double beds and a small sitting area. With only a few suitcases, a coffeepot on a hot plate and rows of clothes on hangers inside the open closet, the visual inventory didn't take long. There was one door, which went to a bathroom only slightly larger than a closet because the shower was outside the cabin in every building but hers.

Joel's shoes scraped against the wood floor as he stepped farther inside. "There's not much here."

She had to take the blame for that one. "I found I have to really limit what they can bring along or some folks come out here with laptops and three suitcases and think someone else will drag it along."

"Very practical." Joel rummaged through a duffel bag on the floor and peeked under the cushions on the loveseat.

Metal screeched as she slid the hangers on the old rod. She spotted a few shirts and extra sneakers on the floor. There wasn't as much as a chest of drawers in the place.

"Blood." Cam didn't add anything else. One word and so deathly serious.

She spun around to find Cam standing by the bed closest to the door. "What?"

Joel got there first, but she was right behind. They all crowded around the bed, staring and unmoving. No one touched anything.

She tried not to state the obvious, but she didn't see anything except crumpled white sheets and a stack of pillows with a clear head indent in them. "What am I looking at?"

Cam nodded in the direction of the bottom of the bed. "The underside of the cover."

Before she could reach over, Joel put out an arm and held her back. Two steps put him at the small table on the other side of the room. He was back in a flash with a pen in his hand.

With the tip, he lifted off the cover and flipped it back. Dark streaks ran about a foot along the underside. Splotches stained the navy blue blanket underneath. The dark shade hid the color. But she knew.

The dizziness hit her full force and the room spun. She would have grabbed for Joel but he'd crouched down to study the bed close up.

"It's not a lot," she said, looking for any positive spin on this horrible find.

"Well, it's more than a few drops," Joel said. "Almost like the spill of a glass of something."

"Are you sure it's blood?" She wanted them to say no, but she knew they wouldn't.

Joel stood back up. "Not without tests, but I think we should assume it is until we see Mark walking around here."

"Maybe he cut himself and didn't tell me?" She was willing to believe anything at this point, so long as the man was healthy and fine.

"What about this gun?" Joel asked.

The question shot out of nowhere and slammed into her with the force of a body blow. They could add the weapon to the list of things suddenly gone missing.

Dread washed over her and she would have sat down hard on the floor, but Joel reached over and settled a hand on her elbow. Technically, he wasn't holding her up, but inside she felt as if he were holding her together.

She tried to explain over the knot of anxiety wedged in her throat. "Unbeknownst to me, he brought it along. He waved it around at dinner, acting like a big shot."

"Guy sounds like a jerk," Cam said.

She felt obligated to defend him on some level. "He was showing off, but my rules are clear. No weapons."

Joel shrugged. "I'm armed."

"So am I," Cam agreed.

They acted as if they were the only ones concerned with safety. "Yeah, well, that makes three of us."

Cam smiled. "Really?"

"We all know the most dangerous person in a situation like this is the nervous novice with the gun." Joel nodded and she took that as approval and kept going. "I can't have people out here with weapons, or sooner or later one of them will shoot off a hand by accident."

He looked around the room. Even opened the bathroom door. "So where is it?"

"What?"

"The gun."

"I have it." She remembered the fight and what she did. "It's in a small lockbox in my cabin." But somehow deep down, she knew it was gone.

Joel stopped in the middle of the room and fixed her with a serious glare. "A hundred bucks says it's missing."

Just went to show how alike they were. She knew, he knew. Heck, maybe even Cam knew.

Still, she had to ask. "Why would you say that?"

Joel didn't hesitate. "Experience."

Chapter Four

Ten minutes later Hope had her leg wound bandaged and cleaned by Joel and carefully kneeled on the floor of her cabin, putting as little weight on the injury as possible. After a quick check under the bed she sat back on her heels and stared up at Joel. "Can I panic now?"

As far as he was concerned, they'd passed that point one missing businessman ago. "Soon."

Joel had come out here as a favor. He'd dragged Cam because he needed a ride. Now they had a full-fledged mess on their hands.

Time was the issue. Mark had been missing for potentially twelve hours or more. That amounted to an emergency. The weather had stayed warm, but the breeze had kicked up and the air carried the scent of rain.

From all accounts Mark wasn't a seasoned hiker. Animals, accidents, falls—the list of dangers went on and on. He could be hurt or worse.

Joel needed to get word to the rest of his team

in Annapolis of the potential issue in West Virginia. They might need search and rescue, or air support, and he sure as hell wanted an answer to who was stalking Hope.

Then there was the bigger problem. The lingering sense of something being off. This should have been a routine assignment for Hope. He understood her dad's worries, and Joel shared them when it came to her safety around a bunch of idiot men in the middle of nowhere, but this felt bigger. Targeted.

Joel didn't like it, and the frown on Cam's face and way he walked around, staring at the floor, suggested he wasn't a fan either. Joel wanted to chalk it up to the mix of guilt and want that pummeled him every time he looked at Hope. She was the one woman who tempted him to give it all up and hunt for a normal ending to his story.

Leaving her was the one time when he'd acted like a complete jerk with a woman and deserved a swift kick. He was lucky she hadn't treated him to one.

But the tic in the back of his neck wasn't about his feelings for her. He loved her until he couldn't see straight. Probably always would. No, this was something else.

He'd been attuned to danger—real danger, not the kind his father manufactured in his sick head—since he joined the military to escape his childhood. He learned to recognize it during his short tenure at Algier Security and honed it at the Defense Intelligence Agency. With Connor's help and the support of the Corcoran Team, he understood not to ignore it and instead figured out how best to handle it.

And he was into it up to his eyeballs now.

"Let's do a weapons check." Joel touched a hand against the gun strapped to his side, then performed a mental rundown of the rest. One at his ankle and the two knives hidden under his clothing, plus the others in the lockbox on the helicopter.

He glanced at Hope. "What do you have?"

"Charlie has a gun." She stood up next to Joel at the side of the bed. "I have a knife and a bow."

"Bow?" Cam broke off from his staring to watch her from across the mattress. "Is that really practical?"

That was the kind of talk that usually led to a demonstration. People underestimated Hope. They saw the pretty face and tight body and decided she must be the type to sit on daddy's piles of money and do nothing.

Joel had made that miscalculation for exactly three minutes before he saw her do a verbal takedown of a guy in her father's office who called her sweetie. Joel had been about to give the guy a lesson in respect, but she'd handled it.

And he'd been hooked ever since. He found other women attractive, but none of them were her. None came close.

He decided to fill Cam in on the nonprivate part. "She was basically a Junior Olympics champion."

"Not just basically." Bending over, she pulled the case out from under the bed and opened it. "Want to see my medals? I have several bows— recurve, long bow and a few compound. You'll have to trust me that I know how to use all of them."

Cam stretched and looked over the bed from his side. "Why did you bring one here? That one's recurve, right?"

She flashed him a smile. "The man knows his hardware."

"Definitely."

"Well, I figured I could show the men how to use it. People generally assume it's easy and have no idea how much strength it takes. And…" Her smile grew to high wattage as she closed the case. "Having a bow and arrows in the room tends to cut down on drunken male idiocy."

That time Cam laughed. "Impressive."

"What do you guys have?" she asked as she sat on the bed.

The laughter in her voice caught Joel in a spell.

Seeing her lighthearted and happy, if only for a few seconds, touched off something inside him.

Near the end they had fought a lot. Then he'd made her cry. He could have gone a lifetime without seeing that, without having her despair rip through him, shredding him from the inside out.

He forced his attention back to the present before the old feelings of guilt swamped him. "Guns, knives." Joel thought about a man tracking her through the woods. "My bare hands."

Her head fell to the side and her hair cascaded over her shoulder. "Strangely, I find that comforting."

A stark silence zipped through the room. It was charged and uncomfortable enough to have him thinking about the big bed right in front of him and Cam squirming as if he wanted to bolt.

He inched toward the door, looking like he was about to do just that. "I should head back to the helicopter and lock it up. Also need to check in with Connor."

Joel nodded. "Fine."

"Who is that?" she asked, seemingly unaware of the firestorm she'd set off in the man she'd once dated.

Joel swallowed a few times and thought about every unsexy thing he could to overwhelm the other thoughts in his head. After a few seconds, his control zapped back to life. "Our boss, Connor Bowen. He runs the Corcoran Team."

"Yeah, like I said, I should contact him." With his hand against the door, Cam appeared to want to do it right then.

Joel didn't disagree. He'd been toying with yelling for the cavalry, but he didn't want to rush everyone in before they conducted a few more easy steps. "Let's see if we can figure this out first. It's still possible we have an annoying businessman acting like a spoiled child."

"How do you explain the gun?" Cam asked.

Joel couldn't. Not without hitting on options that had his temper spiking. That was the problem. "I'm thinking Mark snuck in here and took the box."

"What?" Hope jumped off the bed and wrapped her arms around her body.

"I know that sounds bad, but—"

"While I was sleeping? No way." She rubbed her hands up and down her arms. "Don't you think I'd hear him?"

Cam winced. "Maybe not."

She visibly shivered. "That's just creepy."

"And one of the reasons your dad wanted me here." Joel slid that in there in the hope it would cut off any argument he'd get on the helicopter when they flew out of there the second after they located Mark. Thanks to all she'd described about this retreat so far, he'd leave when she did and not a minute earlier.

She held up a hand. "Don't start."

Looked like her fear or disgust or whatever it was about the lockbox had disappeared. "Your dad is being practical." Joel suspected her father was also engaging in a bit of matchmaking, but Joel decided not to share that thought.

"The word you're looking for is overprotective."

"Hope, I think—"

She turned to Cam. "So, now what?"

He bit his bottom lip in what looked like a poor attempt to block a smile. "We check the helicopter and do a quick search around the campground."

Those priorities worked for Joel. "Cam will question the men here at the campground and maybe see if Charlie knows anything or can give us some direction."

"He knows these woods better than anyone and probably can tell us where someone might hide." She sighed as she shook her head. "I swear if Mark is just being a big baby and staying away because a woman yelled at him, I'm going to hit him."

"Absolutely fine, since nailing him with an arrow is out. Unfortunately," Joel said.

Cam nodded. "Sounds like a reasonable plan."

She let her hand drop to her side again. "But Mark being a jerk still doesn't explain the missing satphone and the stalker."

"You're sure Mark wasn't the one following you?" Man, Joel wanted that to be the answer. It was simple and clean, but he knew life rarely worked that way. Not for him.

"The build was all wrong. Mark is stocky and a bit out of shape. This guy was lean and moved fast."

"I don't like that at all." Cam shook his head as he peeked out the small window next to the cabin's front door. "Heads up—the troops are gathering by the fire pit again. Looks like Charlie is giving them orders."

"I bet Jeff pays attention to Charlie," Hope grumbled.

Cam snorted. "Annoying but at least they're listening. Good to know they can."

Sounded like time had run out. Joel didn't want to spend one more second in planning mode. "Okay, we meet back here in two hours. If we haven't found anything, we start looking in the other cabins."

Hope reached down. "I'll bring—"

No way was Joel dealing with that. "The bow stays here."

"Fine." She got up and joined the men at the door. She glanced at Cam. "I thought you had to be somewhere else today."

He nodded, like he always did. "I'm fine for now."

"Maybe we should all be in on the questioning. I mean, I already checked the woods."

Joel knew that would eat up too much time. "This go-round we'll look for tracks."

"Want me to do that? It's more of my specialty than yours," Cam said.

"We'll be fine."

Cam reached for the doorknob. "I bet."

"Can I have a gun?"

Her question stopped both men. Cam froze and Joel did a quick count to ten. She could handle it, but she was still spooked and he had to be sure she was back in full control before he handed her a loaded gun. Still… "No."

"Can you shoot?" Cam asked.

"Been practicing since I was ten."

Joel wasn't having this conversation right now. He reached around and shoved the door open, bringing the warm breeze inside. "Shooting a person is different."

Her head snapped back. "Are we doing that?"

He hoped not. "Maybe."

"And you would know how hard that is."

He glanced at her over his shoulder. "Yes, I would."

THEY'D CROSSED OUT of sight of the campground before Hope broached the difficult subject. Actually, about a hundred feet away she opened her mouth and then closed it again, focusing on the sway of branches against the increasing wind and the clomp of their feet against the ground.

Later they hit the point where she could see sunlight up ahead and knew the helicopter sat a short distance away. She didn't hold back. "Are we going to talk about it?"

He stopped scanning the trees and large expanse of forest around them to spare her a glance. "About what?"

Men were clueless. "Us."

He exhaled. "Hope—"

"I know. You don't have to list off the reasons why we should pretend we've never slept together."

"I never said that."

"You act like it."

"And, for the record, it was more than sex."

"Was it?" She asked even though she couldn't stand to hear him dismiss their relationship as unimportant—again.

True, they hadn't been together in what felt like forever. She'd convinced herself she didn't care and could move on, but seeing him made her realize how untrue that was.

He picked a leaf off a branch that nearly whacked him in the face. "We can't do this now."

The world around her barely registered. Not when this topic came up.

She'd heard all of the excuses. They ran through her mind on constant play. They spilled out of her now before she could call them back. "This is the wrong time. I'm the wrong guy. You deserve better. My background is a mess. My job is dangerous."

He stopped. "Excuse me?"

"Have you invented more reasons? I've heard all of those, and none of them sent *me* running."

"Wow."

She debated storming ahead, leaving him floundering, but refrained. Childish wasn't the answer when what she really wanted was for him to treat her the way a woman deserved to be treated. "Imagine how I felt as you ticked off that list, or some version of it, day after day. You always had a new reason to push away and leave, but you never found one to stay."

"That's not true."

She knew it was because she had lived it. "All those months ago I asked you to move in with me since you were basically staying there every night anyway, and you flew out of town on a business trip the next morning instead of giving me an answer."

"That was legitimate."

"Joel, come on."

The leaf disappeared as Joel crushed it inside

his clenched fist. "Your father said you were dating again."

Her gaze slipped back up to his. "What?"

"No?"

The conversation had her mind spinning. Her dad still talked with Joel? And since when was her dating life up for discussion? Not that she really had one. She struggled through a few setups from friends and had a perfectly nice time with a guy from her climbing club.

Handsome men, fun places and she didn't experience so much as a spark. Not even a tiny nibble of interest.

But that's not where her mind went when Joel asked the question. It zoomed right to her nightmare scenario. The one where he walked away and found someone else. Where the truth turned out to be not that he wasn't ready to make a commitment but that he didn't want to make one to *her*.

"Are *you?*" Two simple words, but it actually hurt her to say them.

"I didn't leave you so I could date other women. My decision wasn't about being a playboy." His voice rose and anger slipped in as he spoke.

As if he had a right to be upset about the fallout. "Well, I guess that's good to know."

Instead of standing around arguing, she headed in the direction of the helicopter. This was a waste of time and they had more important things to worry about than her broken heart.

Joel grabbed her arm before she got more than three feet. "Hey, wait up."

She didn't shake out of his grip, though she could have because his hold was more gentle than confining. Seeing the pain in his dark eyes killed off any thought of pulling back anyway.

He closed in, bringing his body within a few breaths of hers. "You know I'm telling the truth, right?"

"I know you had a lot of excuses. Still do." And she couldn't hear them again. Not and still function.

"Hope, look…I want…"

"What?" She heard the pleading in her voice.

His eyes closed and when they opened again the wary expression hadn't faded. "Maybe we should stick to finding Mark."

Just like that, the mood changed. Something snapped and the tension that had been building blew away.

Because he seemed to want an out, she gave him one. Maybe a change of topic made sense. There had been so much pain and disappointment, so many tears. She needed her head in the game and her mind on Mark. "Fine. Why are we headed back to the helicopter instead of following tracks?"

"I want to check in at work."

"And?" Joel's face went blank and she wasn't falling for it. "Oh, please. Maybe I didn't see you walking out on me, but I do know you. Part of you, and you are fixated and worried."

"I didn't leave you—"

"Joel."

His hand dropped. "Okay, yes. I'm concerned."

"You're admitting it?"

"You deserve that much." He motioned with his head for them to start walking again. "This is your job, and I think something is very wrong here."

The honesty flooded her with relief. "Good."

"Why good?"

"Sharing even that much is a big step for you."

"I thought you'd be happy I left." His voice dropped to a near whisper. "Back then, I mean."

The words stunned her and she stumbled. She stared at him, thinking he had to be playing a sick joke, even though that wasn't his style. But he looked ahead, not even blinking.

"You've got to be kidding." She was about to pull him to a stop when a crack echoed through the trees. Dirt kicked up a few feet away from her, and birds swooped out of the trees in a rush.

"Get down!" His full body smacked into her before he finished talking.

The ground rushed up and she put out a hand to stop the free fall. Her legs twisted with his and the second before she slammed into the ground he turned them.

Landing on his side with a grunt, he absorbed the majority of their combined body weight on his shoulder. His body bounced and she tried to move away and let him brace for impact, but he curled her body into his. Still, the jolt rattled her teeth and she heard him swear under his breath.

She could taste dirt and feel sharp sticks jabbing into her bare legs and ripping off her bandage. Her mind finally focused and the sounds of the forest came rushing back. "Joel—"

"Don't move."

It had sounded like… But it couldn't be. "What was that?" She whispered the question as she frantically looked around.

Before she could scramble to her feet, he shoved her against the ground and covered her body with his. His fingers slipped into her hair as he held her down. She heard a steady stream of reassuring words, but they barely registered over the fear and panic pounding through her.

She expected shouts and more pops. When nothing came, she glanced up. His gaze scanned the area, and his gun was up and ready. She swallowed hard at the vulnerability of their position. Right there on her makeshift path with nothing covering them or blocking their view in any direction.

"A gunshot." He was so close the words vibrated against the side of her head.

Adrenaline pumped through her, and her heartbeat hammered in her ears so loudly she thought for sure she'd give away their position. "Where did it come from?"

"I'm more worried about who and how many." He shifted his weight until most of it fell away to her side. "Stay under me."

"Are you wearing a bulletproof vest?"

"Didn't think I'd need one."

She waited for the attacker to rush them. Listened for another shot. "I can't hear or see anything."

"I need to get to the helicopter."

A vision of him running and getting shot hit her with the force of a crashing train. The horror of it stole her breath and had her fingernails digging into the dirt. "No."

"I have a vest and binoculars in there." He slipped farther off her. "Other weapons."

"You can't risk going into the open."

With barely a touch he moved them to the left. She felt his deep inhale before he rolled them over and stopped close to a large tree trunk. He tapped the back of her legs. "Curl up."

When the world finally stopped spinning she looked up and saw rough bark right in front of her face and threw a hand out to touch the surface. "What are we doing?"

"You are going to make yourself as small as possible." He gave the orders without looking at her. His head kept moving as he glanced around them. "Then you're not to move."

"You can't—"

"I'm serious. You move and I will come back, which is more of a threat to me than racing over there." With a hand between her shoulder blades, he lowered her closer to the ground. "Stay down."

Before she could grab on or call him back, he was gone. In a crouch, zigzagging he broke through the last line of trees. He hugged close to the helicopter as he lifted a hand. The door must have stuck or his angle was off because she saw him pulling and tugging.

With all her concentration, she focused on him. Her teeth clicked together as terror spun through her. She waited for footsteps to fall and a hand to pull her up. The only thing that kept her from screaming was watching Joel. Even as her vision blurred around the edges, she stared.

After some fiddling and a yank, he got the door open and bonelessly slipped inside. One minute his dark hair provided a beacon and the next he was gone.

Her breath hiccupped in her chest as she fought the urge to run after him. She'd just decided to do that when she saw his head again. He held binoculars and swept his gaze over the forest. The door inched open and he was off again, this time running toward her.

He slid in beside her, kicking up twigs and leaves around her. He held up a vest. "Put this on."

"You need it."

"I think the person is gone, but I don't want to risk you getting shot."

When he continued to hold the vest, she took it and slid it on. The way he stared at her with that I-can-wait-all-day expression had her adjusting the straps and securing it tighter to her body. "Happy?"

"Not really."

That made two of them. She looked at the binoculars. They weren't the standard bird watching kind.

"Do they do something special?" She half hoped they functioned as a grenade launcher. She'd be satisfied with any weapon that could protect them all and get them out of there fast.

"Increased magnification and brightness. Plus the universal mil reticle." He spit all that out without lowering the glasses.

"Um, okay."

"The last is a special feature snipers use." This time he looked at her. "It allows for better targeting and range estimates."

The techno-jargon filled her with a strange sense of relief. It was as if they had walked right into his wheelhouse. She was fine to stay there with him.

Despite all their personal troubles, she never doubted his competency on the job. He was the man any sane person would want on her team when things fell apart. Now qualified.

Still, the sniper talk had her attention. "I don't know most of the words you just used."

"It means—"

She put a hand on his arm. "Don't explain. I'm just happy you know what you're talking about."

He nodded. "We need to get back."

The comment started a new round of thundering in her chest. "How do we know it's safe?"

"I'll feel better when we're in the cabins."

She'd feel better in her town house. "Any chance your team is on the way?"

"I called them. Yes."

"That's good news." But she noticed he wasn't smiling and didn't look one ounce more relieved than he was before he crawled into the helicopter for reinforcements. "Right?"

"I'll explain later."

Something inside her shriveled. "I was afraid you'd say that."

Chapter Five

Tony Prather had no idea who or what Connor Bowen was, but the man was on his way up to the executive floor of Baxter Industries. Tony glanced out of his conference room window to the Washington, D.C., skyline in the distance. His Rosslyn office had a view across the Potomac River to Georgetown.

He'd worked hard for his position with the big office, complete with private executive bathroom and two administrative assistants. He wasn't accustomed to jumping when others issued orders. If anyone other than Rafe Algier had phoned in from a trip abroad and asked, Tony would have had someone on his staff offer an excuse and insist he couldn't be disturbed.

But Algier Security had sent work Baxter's way, and back when business was floundering Rafe had provided some much-needed contracts and personnel to help keep Baxter's doors open. Tony had a strong loyalty to the man. It was why he had agreed to hire his daughter for the executive retreat.

Well, part of the reason. Tony didn't get where he was by being soft. His obligation didn't pass from Rafe to his daughter.

Tony had taken over the reins of Baxter after a coup by the old board of directors. When the bottom fell out of the financial markets and business dried up, the old president and chief executive officer lost the confidence of everyone from shareholders to the management staff. Tony stepped in and got the place running again. He expanded the company's services.

They no longer just provided tech and personnel to government agencies. Now his people staffed Fortune 500 companies and smaller businesses. Anyone who didn't want to pay employee benefits and could afford Baxter's bills was welcome.

But that didn't mean he had time to babysit some guy with an agenda. And Rafe hadn't taken the time to explain anything, which ticked Tony off. He had other worries. All his plans, those tenuous pieces he needed to come together and fit just so, were breaking down. He had a partner he didn't trust and a problem he needed to fix.

He'd rebuilt it all and couldn't afford to have it crumble now. Not when he was so close to the end.

The phone on the credenza buzzed and he gave

the okay for one of his assistants to usher in their unwanted guest. Better to get it over with and move on.

The man who stepped through the glass doors and stopped was not what Tony expected. Tall with dark hair, he wore a business suit minus the jacket. But that's not what stuck out. It was the lethal look. The man appeared ready for battle. So did the muscled man behind him.

Earlier, Rafe had talked about needing to get in touch with his daughter. Tony had barely listened because the mere mention of Hope Algier's name at this point in the process had Tony speed dialing his partner. Not that he could get through.

"I'm Connor Bowen." The man motioned to the guy with him. "This is Davis Weeks."

"Gentlemen." Tony nodded because that's what protocol demanded.

Inside, his rage boiled. He'd prepared for one of them. Bowen was president and owner of something called the Corcoran Team. The Internet and paperwork trail pointed to a threat assessment group. The kind of team that taught businessmen how not to get kidnapped while playing in Mexico and made plans for getting them out when they did.

All aboveboard and clean, but Tony recognized an off-the-books undercover operation when he saw one. And that had his interest. So did this

Weeks character. The guy hadn't blinked and if the bulge under his jacket was an indication, he'd somehow snuck a gun through security.

"I'm Tony Prather." He motioned toward the seats across the conference table from him. "I was told only one of you would be coming."

"Davis is my second in command. He understands the situation."

Because Tony needed to know what that was, he played along. Still, this was his turf, so he took the lead. "What can I help you with?"

Connor leaned forward with his elbows folded on the table in front of him. "There's a problem at your management retreat."

A stark silence followed the statement. Tony guessed that was the point. Drop the bombshell and then assess his reaction.

He had no intention of giving them anything. "Meaning?"

This time Davis spoke up. "One of your executives is missing and there's been some other trouble."

"This is a get-away-from-it-all retreat. How would you know what's happening there?" Tony had been trying to check in, and the messages he'd received made no sense.

Connor's hand dropped to the table, and his fingers drummed on the top. "Some of my people are there."

The information would have been good to know before now. Funny how Rafe had left that out. "Some?"

"More than one."

The steady thumping touched off a headache. Tony had enough of that right now. "Care to tell me why?"

Connor shrugged. "As a favor to Rafe."

Looked like he wasn't the only one indebted to Rafe Algier in some way. Tony wasn't sure how he felt about that. The idea of the old man moving the chess pieces around, using them all, had Tony balling his hands into fists on his lap.

"Does he know his daughter is tangled up in this?" Tony had put her there for a reason and now it could all unravel thanks to this Corcoran Team and Rafe's meddling.

"Not all the details," Connor said. "Rafe is breaking away from his meetings in Vietnam and should be taking off soon to head back."

"This is that serious?" Tony noticed only the one in charge talked. Tony appreciated the chain of command as much as the next guy, but the silence from Davis proved unnerving. The guy sat and stared.

A lesser man would get twitchy and start talking. If that was the plan, these two sorely underestimated him. Tony Prather could not be intimidated. Others had tried and failed at using that tactic.

He hadn't won his current position by shaking hands and saying yes all the time. He'd pushed his predecessor out and never looked back. He'd won the office and the hot young wife. That's what he did—he won.

Davis finally shifted in his chair. The movement was slight, but it had the focus switching to him. "You didn't ask which executive is missing."

Tony knew all about Mark's situation. Knew and was watching, but these two didn't need that information. "I'm assuming whoever it was got lost on a hike and this isn't really a big deal."

Davis and Connor exchanged glances. Connor started talking again after Davis nodded. "Right before I spoke with one of my team members earlier today, he came under fire."

Tony was more interested in which man was in charge than about this conversation. Still, he had a role to play. "You mean—"

"Gunshots." Connor exhaled as if explaining bored him. "At the camp."

Time for concern. Hitting the appropriate level would be the trick. Tony went with pushing his chair back and reaching for the phone. "I need to get them all out."

"My people are working on that." Connor glanced at the phone and continued when Tony returned it to the cradle. "Once the weather breaks we'll move in."

Not the response Tony had expected. He figured they'd rush in and rescue, or whatever they normally did. The change in expectations and protocol sent a new push of adrenaline rushing through him. "Send in the park rangers. Do something."

Davis's eyes narrowed. "If we didn't have a 'shots fired' situation, maybe, but we can't risk putting anyone else in danger."

All reasonable answers. But Tony couldn't shake the feeling he was being sized up and checked out. That was probably fair because he was playing the same game at the moment.

Right now he needed to know their real plan. He guessed they wouldn't share most of it, but maybe he could drag out something. "So, what's next?"

Connor thumped his fingertips even louder. "My guys will secure the scene until I can get emergency personnel in there."

Tony glanced down but Connor didn't stop. "And in the meantime what happens to my executive?"

"We try to find him," Davis said.

Definitive and solid. Tony looked for a chink in their show and didn't see one. The routine came off as practiced but appropriate. He had to admit a part of him was a little impressed. These two could give lessons in remaining cool and detached.

"Should I contact his family or at least notify the board?" he asked.

"Let's see where we are tomorrow." Connor stood up. "We need to get back, but I'll keep you updated."

"Absolutely." Tony reached across the table and shook their hands. "Thanks for coming in."

Connor nodded. "I'm sorry I don't have more definitive news."

"I'm going to continue to believe this is a case of wandering away from camp and not a disaster."

"Except for the gunshots." Davis delivered the line in a flat voice. He didn't say much, but what he did force out came with a punch.

Tony admired the skill. "That could be hunters, anything."

"I have a conference call scheduled with search and rescue. You're welcome to listen in." Connor slipped a business card out of the pocket of his dress shirt and set it on the table.

Tony left it there. "I appreciate that. My assistant can give you all my contact information, including the home numbers."

"Good." Connor headed to the door with Davis right behind him.

At the last minute, Davis turned around again. "Mark."

That fast the air sucked out of the room. "Excuse me?"

"Your missing executive. His name is Mark Callah." For the first time, Davis smiled.

Tony found it more intimidating than the staring. "Connor already told me that."

"Did I?" he asked.

Tony stuck with the story because he refused to believe he'd messed up and not asked what would be the obvious question. This was a trap and he would not fall into it. "Yes."

"I'll call in a few hours." After one last up and down, Connor left, taking Davis with him.

JOEL TRIED TO think of a way the past hour could have gone worse. Hope wanted to have "the talk" in the middle of a potential missing persons case. Add in bad weather, gunshots and no answers, and Joel wanted to yank all of them out of there and go home.

He might have done so if the flight wasn't dangerous and he didn't have a missing camper lost out in the unforgiving woods somewhere. Still, the idea of shoving Hope on the helicopter and telling Cam to fly her to safety was compelling. The fact that she would refuse wasn't Joel's biggest concern. He could—would—make her if that's what he had to do to keep her safe.

He had left her to give her a normal life. Forfeiting that now was not okay with him. Not after all he'd lost.

They stepped into camp. When Joel saw the flat expression on Cam's face, he knew something was wrong.

"What's going on?" Joel called out.

Cam joined them at the line where the trees met the open space. "Perry's officially missing."

Hope let out a stifled gasp. "You've got to be kidding. We're missing two now?"

"Charlie last saw him in the kitchen area around breakfast, but there's no sign of him at all." Cam kicked the dirt under his feet.

Joel tried to ignore the uncharacteristic shifting, but it made him nervous. "His bed?"

"Slept in and all of his stuff is in his cabin." Cam looked up. "Good news is we don't have blood this time."

"I can't believe that now qualifies as good news." She leaned against Joel.

Cam shrugged. "Well, it's not as bad as it could be."

Without thinking, Joel put a hand against her lower back and brought her in closer to his side. Despite the warm weather, her skin felt cold and the chill seeped through his clothes to his skin.

The wind had cooled, but not enough to explain the shivers running through her.

Cam's gaze shot to the lack of space between Joel and Hope, then back up again. "Jeff and Lance are pretty jumpy. Charlie is on the side of that last cabin, walking them through some camping tips."

As far as Joel was concerned, that was the sort of thing that should have happened before the retreat started. "Now?"

"I did that before," she said.

Cam waved off the concern. "I think he's trying to keep them calm."

"Well." Hope rubbed her hands up and down her arms. "Maybe I should listen in then."

Joel knew she was suffering from a case of nerves. She didn't need a class on wilderness survival. In their months apart she'd taken more and more risks, climbing higher mountains and guiding tours thousands of feet into the air. He hated the idea of her up there, but he knew she loved it. And they were no longer together, so he limited his complaints to her dad. Not that they worked.

The corner of Cam's mouth lifted as his gaze wandered over Hope and Joel. "What happened to you two?"

"Get ready for more bad news," she said.

Joel didn't feel like playing games, so he skipped right to it. "Someone shot at us."

Cam's mouth fell into a flat line again. "What?"

She blew out a long, labored breath. "One shot but it had us ducking."

Cam nodded. "I'd think so."

"Well then." She stepped out of Joel's hold. "I should go do some work."

Joel admired her courage to not sit in a corner and rock. Most people would, but not her. But he still worried about her shell-shocked expression and wavering voice. "You okay?"

Cam cut off any chance of getting her to stay. "I need to talk with you."

Even though he wanted to follow her, Joel let Hope go but not before one more reminder. "You need to check your knee and put on another bandage."

She nodded but didn't say anything. That didn't stop him from staring. He watched her walk across the campground, ignoring the gentle swish of her hips and not breaking focus until he saw her stop next to Charlie in the distance.

Cam took a few steps and came to stand beside Joel. "The others were with me the whole time. None of these three could have taken the shot at you."

Joel had already come to that conclusion. Ruling some people out narrowed their choices. He didn't like any of the remaining ones. "Then we need to deal with the very real possibility either Mark or Perry, or both, are at the bottom or this."

"There's another possibility." Cam matched Joel's stance and stared at the others as well. "We could have an unknown out here stalking people."

There it was. The worst possible answer. An unknown meant they were dealing with a surprise. The person could be on drugs or unstable or just enjoy killing.

Joel didn't want Hope near any of those types. "I've been trying not to think about that option."

"It would explain the gunshots." Cam stared at him then. "I'm guessing you didn't see anyone."

"Nothing. The guy totally got the drop on me."

Cam made a face. "Weird."

"I know." Joel understood the surprise. He wasn't the type to miss someone sneaking up on him.

He'd been training for surveillance his entire life. He had tracked and practiced from the day after he turned seven and his dad insisted the family go totally off the grid. Maybe those early lessons grew out of his father's sick paranoia, but he instilled a sense of caution and taught certain skills. The same skills that served Joel well as he passed from one position to another in the intelligence community.

That likely meant the attacker was equally well trained. Joel hated that prospect.

Cam let out an impressive line of profanity. "What did Connor say?"

"He's on the way and will bring everyone from the forest rangers to the local police with him."

Connor was solid that way. No questions or explanations needed. Joel was on a few days of leave, but he knew if he sent up the red flag, the team would come running.

He'd missed that in his other employment positions and throughout most of his life. He didn't know the sensation of someone putting it all out there for him. His mom had died before he could really know her, and his father's idea of love was handing over a rifle and teaching him to shoot.

Now Joel needed to fill Cam in on the bad part. Joel owed him that since Cam was only out here as a favor. "One problem."

"I'm not sure we need another."

"A storm is moving in."

"Of course it is." Cam groaned. "There's always a storm right when you don't need one."

"Connor can't get in until morning, and even then that's not a guarantee." Joel doubted the timetable anyway. He could smell the rain in the air and feel the dampness on his skin, even though not a single drop had fallen. But Connor talked about violent thunderstorms rolling in and Joel guessed they were headed this way. At the very least, the weather grounded planes. "So, we hunker down."

"I was afraid you were going to say that."

And it was about to get worse, so Joel braced. "I say we do a quick meal, stick together until dark or rain or whatever comes first. Then those of us with weapons split up and bunk with the others."

Cam's mouth broke out into a full grin. "Let me guess which cabin you'll be in."

Knowing the ribbing could go on for hours, Joel ignored the first shot. "You with Lance and we'll let Charlie handle Jeff."

"And you with Hope."

Joel rolled his eyes. "Yes."

"You ready to tell me what happened with her before you came to Corcoran?"

He still battled with the details. He couldn't lay it out there. Not after he was barely holding together from Hope's insistence they pick at it. "No."

Cam nodded and Joel thought he might be in the clear. They needed to concentrate and—

"I'm thinking you'll need practice," Cam said, breaking into Joel's thoughts.

He bit back a groan. "Meaning?"

"I don't know much about women—"

"True."

"—but even I know there's no way you're going to spend the night together without the topic of your relationship implosion coming up." Cam ended the comment with a knowing look.

Joel ignored the description of his upcoming evening, even though he wanted to deny it. "We're grown-ups."

The nodding came back. Cam did love to nod. "I'm guessing that's what she'll say before she demands an explanation."

"What makes you think we didn't work this out already?"

Joel wished. He wanted to fix the damage and move on. Because forgetting her appeared to be out of the question, he'd settle for a healthy parting. One that took away the sadness that moved into her eyes when she talked about them.

"What was the word you used earlier on her?" Cam looked up and closed one eye, as if he were pretending to mull it over. "Oh, right. Experience."

"We're the same age and I doubt you're any better at this women stuff than I am." Joel hoped for Cam's sake that wasn't true.

"But I wouldn't be dumb enough to let that woman go."

This time Joel nodded. There was that.

Chapter Six

Hope tried busywork to calm the nerves somersaulting in her stomach. With her knee bandaged and everyone tucked away, she tried to settle in. She drew down the bed covers, then drew them up again and tucked them around the pillows.

Next came sitting. She dropped onto the mattress and looked around the cabin. It was a utilitarian space with dark furniture and windows that rattled when a strong gust of air blew in, like right now. Her space measured about twenty square feet more than the others and included an inside shower.

That was pretty much a prerequisite for her on a retreat like this. She'd rather go without than risk flashing half the camp. Here she didn't have to make the choice.

But she had bigger problems ahead. Well, one. Joel.

He stood with his broad back to her and stared out the small window next to the door. He wore the same pants he was wearing when he'd landed.

Charlie had lent him a clean T-shirt. The rest of Joel's clothes sat in his bag on the helicopter. He insisted another run was too risky in light of the guy practicing his sniper skills out here.

Rain pelted the windows and had kept them all trapped inside for the past few hours. Now the sun had gone down and the ceiling light in the center of the room highlighted everything, including all six-feet-whatever of him.

The ruffled dark hair and scruff around his chin had always been her favorite look for him. Made him look rugged and reminded her of his sexy ability to handle almost any situation.

"We've slept in the same room before." He made the comment without looking at her.

She had to smile. "Many times, but we were dating back then."

Sometimes she thought the phrase "eyes in the back of his head" was invented to describe him. He always seemed to have a clue about what was happening around him, even if he acted like he didn't care or his eyes were closed.

"True." He turned but didn't move one inch closer. "And no one was shooting at us."

"Now look at us." She sat on her hands to keep from fidgeting or waving them around.

His gaze bounced to her lap, then back to her face. "I'll sleep on the floor."

Interesting how he had his lines and she had

hers. Having him nod off during the next shoot-out was not her idea of a good time. "You'll sleep in the bed with me."

"That's not a great idea."

Oh, she knew that. His scent, his arms. The way he wrapped his body around hers and pulled her in tight. All dangerous for her self-control. "Agreed."

He held out a hand. "Then throw me a pillow and—"

"But it's still happening."

With that his arm dropped to his side again. "You go to my head."

And he didn't look particularly happy about the idea. His face stayed blank and his eyes flat. He froze in place and looked as likely to bolt as he was to take a step closer.

The words both freeing and empty went to her head and stuck there. "What does that mean?"

"I've never been attracted to a woman the way I'm attracted to you." He pushed away from the door and walked across the room.

With each step, his hiking boots fell quietly against the hard floor. The cabin walls creaked and thunder drummed in the distance. The harder the winds and heavier the sheets of rain, the more she waited for the outside to storm in. The sturdy structures held, but a dribble leaked in at the back left corner near the open closet.

All she could focus on was the soft tap of his steps until he stopped in front of her. With only a foot separating them, she could smell him. Feel the weight of his gaze upon her.

As she stood, her gaze traveled over his flat stomach and the smooth muscles under his damp tee. "So, naturally, you left me."

"Normal doesn't work for me."

How many times had she heard that excuse? It appeared to be his favorite, which made it her least. "You say that often enough for it to be your motto."

"The way I was raised..." He broke off and shook his head. "Look, things can work for a little while but that's it."

There it was. The blanket statement that ended it all. The sentiment would have been sweetly misguided if it hadn't driven them apart. He believed. It amounted to nonsense talk, but in his head he viewed it as truth.

Shame that on this one issue he ignored the reality that life could be better than what he was handed. "How do you know?"

His eyes narrowed. "What?"

"How many long-term relationships have you had?" She steeled her body for the verbal blow. She had a theory and put it out there, hoping she'd turn out to be right.

"We should talk about something else." He started to pivot.

"I'll narrow it down for you." She spoke louder and put a hand on his arm to hold him there. "Did you ever live with a woman?"

He blinked a few times. "Just you, and that was informal."

The relief crashing over her nearly knocked her down. "Ever date one woman for more than three months in a row?"

He didn't hesitate. "You."

The last of the tension whooshed out of her. Even though she seemed to be the only one fighting for them, at least he refrained from using her weakness for him against her. "Then you have no idea what you could or couldn't do long term."

"I didn't go to school until I was eleven." He folded his hand over hers where it lay against her arm.

"Do you think that's a test for something?" The rain cast dampness over everything and had her shivering, but his touch sent warmth spiraling through her.

"Yes, for everything."

His palm brought the heat back to her limbs. "All it says to me is your father was a sick man, which I already knew. He grew paranoid and scary and died from a brain tumor. You didn't hide that from me."

His hand squeezed hers. "That wasn't really an option since your father had my information and knew."

Not a surprise. Her father specialized in collecting information. The more confidential and harder to find, the more he liked hunting it down. He was a specific type of person. The same type as Joel.

"Believe it or not, he didn't hand me your personnel file," she said.

This time Joel smiled and life sparked behind those serious eyes. "I bet he tried."

"Yes." He'd lectured, done everything but make a pros and cons list about Joel.

Not that her dad would put anything on the con list. He loved Joel like a son and wanted him to be *the* one for her. Dad had never been subtle on that point.

"Why didn't you take it?" Joel asked.

That was easy. "I wanted to learn everything about you in the *normal* way. Date like normal people. Eat together like normal people. Find out about each other like normal people."

"I remember our first date." His free hand went to her hair. He slid it forward and weaved his fingers through.

"Italian food. We ate for three hours."

He wrapped a lock around his forefinger. "I was done in ten minutes, but I moved a few stray pieces around on my plate because I wanted to be with you as long as possible."

Her heart did a perfect backflip. "When did that stop?"

The sadness moved back into his eyes as his thumb traced her lower lip. "Never."

"So, you left me for a job." The words stuck in her chest, but she shoved them out, letting them rip and tear as they went.

"Yes."

The word hit her like a punch. "And then you left that job for the one you have now."

She didn't understand that choice. He had confessed how much he wanted the position at the Defense Intelligence Agency, how he needed to be available to come and go. That the work would be dangerous and the hours impossible. He'd pick up and leave and couldn't tell her...so they should move on from each other.

The memory of how easy it had been for him to deliver the horrible news still haunted her. She'd begged and he'd walked away. Never looked back.

But now she saw a different man. This Joel didn't celebrate leaving her. When he looked at her he acted as if the need crushed him. She just wished he could see it. She wished he was willing to do something to fix them.

His chest rose and fell on heavy breaths as his

fingertips brushed against her cheek. "The DIA job was a mistake."

Not the answer she expected. Not really the question in her mind either. "Was leaving me a mistake?"

He closed his eyes for the briefest of seconds "Hope, don't—"

She stopped his words by putting her palms on either side of his face. "Kiss me."

"No." There was no heat behind the word.

"Why?"

"I won't stop."

She leaned in closer, letting her breath mingle with his. "You will. We'll kiss and then we'll get in that bed and sleep."

"You have more faith in my control than I do."

He acted like this was easy for her. Like she wasn't waging a battle to win *them* back. "You would never touch me without my permission."

"Of course not." His hands went to her waist and with a tug her chest pressed against his.

"You don't have it." She dropped a small kiss on his chin. "You would have to earn it."

"You're killing me." His face went into her hair, and his mouth nuzzled her ear.

The brush of air across her skin sent a tremor racing down her spine. The shiver brought with it an ache. A need to be near him. "That pretty face of yours isn't enough for me to drop my common sense."

He chuckled. "Good to know."

"But you could—"

"Kiss you."

He didn't ask for permission a second time or for an order from her. He dipped his head and his lips touched hers. The kiss slipped from sweet to hot before one second could pass to the next.

Fire rolled over her as her nerve endings sparked to life. Her hands tingled. She wanted to crawl in closer and never let him go.

His mouth passed over hers and a grumble built in the back of his throat. He kissed her hard and deep and kicked life into every fantasy she'd ever had of him, every memory she held as sacred.

When he lifted his head the room continued to spin. Her fingers gripped his back, and her pulse thumped in her ears.

With a groan, he leaned his forehead against hers. "You think we can stop cold after a few more of those?"

She could barely catch her breath. It rushed out of her in huge shuddering gasps. "We're going to stop because we need our rest, although I bet you're going to stay up most of the night keeping watch."

"You do know me." He lifted his head and kissed her again, this one short yet determined.

She pulled her head back before either one of them was tempted to deepen it. "Parts."

He sighed, exhaled, treated her to the whole "you win" vibe males had. "There hasn't been anyone else."

Deep down she knew that. He couldn't look at her the way he did and then run home to someone else. He wasn't that guy. It wasn't his 89 style.

Knowing that and knowing the reality of how people worked were two different things. People moved on. They had sex and fell in love. He was worth it and believed to her soul he eventually would believe it, too. He was a catch, whether or not he realized that.

"But there will be. Someone else, I mean." She whispered the phrase because it hurt to say it louder.

"No."

The quickness of his comeback had the hope inside her surging again. "I'm wondering if you'll ever trust me enough to stay."

He cupped her cheek. "It's not about trust."

That's the part he never got. If he really loved her and trusted her to accept him for who and what he was, he wouldn't run. He'd stay and fight.

But he didn't and she could feel him slipping away again.

She covered his hand with hers and stepped back, breaking the connection between them. "Yeah, it is."

THE CHAIR WITH its thin cushion turned out to be pretty uncomfortable. The longer Joel sat there, the more his lower back ached. But he didn't plan to move. Not when the seat gave him the best view of her on the other side of the cabin.

He'd found a small lamp stuck in the corner. With it plugged in across the room from the bed and the shade turned toward the ceiling, it bathed the cabin in a soft light. Most of the small space stayed hidden in shadows, but he could see her face.

Lying there with his arms wrapped around her and that body pressed against his for hours had amounted to slow torture. Hours with her curled up so close. The position, the smell of her hair, it all brought the memories back.

Eighteen months ago she'd handed him the key to her apartment and temptation pulled at him to stay. He'd wanted to grab it and try to make it work. He'd toyed with the idea even though he always promised himself years ago he would never drag another person into his messed up life.

He'd switched jobs and got antsy. He craved the outdoors and didn't have time for the bar scene. Even now he lived in the third-floor crash pad of the Corcoran Team headquarters instead of taking the time to find his own place.

Committing came hard for him—to a job, to a plan, to a path that got him somewhere other than slinging a gun while hiding in the woods. He didn't want to settle in and act the way other people did.

His time in the DIA ended when his boss accused him of selling the team out for cash. The man pivoted right off the charge, almost immediately, and Joel didn't do anything wrong, but the damage was done in Joel's mind.

He'd spent a lifetime bouncing around from obligation to obligation and hadn't stayed anywhere for long. His upbringing had taught him to keep ties to a minimum and possessions to almost nothing. He'd tried to break the cycle, but since he didn't even have a closet to his name, he'd clearly failed.

Still, the Corcoran Team had changed him, given him focus and a place. Connor set down enough rules to promote excellence and consistency but didn't micromanage. That balance let Joel breathe.

In exchange, he filled any role the team needed. He honed his tech skills to make his work indispensable and spent hours at the shooting range perfecting his game. He refused to disappoint the members who had become closer than family to him.

Then there was Hope. She was everything he wanted. Smart, athletic, driven and fun. She didn't get caught up in her father's wealth and wasn't impressed with fancy cars or the usual trappings. Her one weakness was for big comfy beds stacked with pillows. He smiled at the memory of the bedroom in her town house. A man could fall into it and get lost in the mass of blankets.

Of course, most things about her made him smile. She didn't pester. She understood the concept of work secrets and didn't push. Her easy acceptance had almost made it harder on him. He'd kept waiting for the bottom to drop, and the tension built with each day it didn't. Another sick cycle he couldn't figure out how to break.

"I can feel you staring at me." Her sleepy voice floated through the room.

Even in the limited light he could see her eyes remained shut and her body buried in the covers. She claimed the whistle of the wind helped her sleep. Could be, but the humidity hadn't faded and until it did he'd prefer to sleep without clothing, and that could not happen with her if he hoped to keep his "hands off" promise.

He watched her mouth curve into a smile and tried to cut off whatever was happening in her head to put it there. "You should be asleep."

She shifted and made a sexy little grumbling sound. "With you."

"Being even this close to you is killing me."

Her eyes popped open. "Good."

Funny how she liked that word, especially when she used it for instances he found to be the exact opposite of good. "Why?"

She lifted herself up on her elbow. "You should suffer."

The words stung. They didn't slice through him as they once would have, likely because of her softer delivery this time, but they bit. "Because I hurt you."

She shook her head, and her hair fell over her shoulder. "Because you still are."

Debating how far to go, he decided to give her the truth. Man up and take the deep plunge.

He leaned over and balanced his elbows on his knees. "You know I love you, right?"

"Yes."

Her expression didn't change, but he thought he saw a hint of satisfaction mirrored in her eyes. This woman… "That was easy."

After a sigh, she rolled her eyes. Ran through the entire "men are clueless" list of gestures he'd seen before. "Joel Kidd, nothing about you is easy."

Not really a point he could argue with, so he

stuck with rubbing his hands together where they hung between his knees. "Fair enough."

"Come to bed." Her gaze roamed over his tee and down his bare legs.

He wore his boxer briefs and was ten seconds away from stripping them off. Which made his answer very easy. "I should ride out the night over here."

Instead of taking the hint and gathering up the blanket around her again, she threw back the sheet and patted the mattress. "Do it here."

He should have said no. Insisted they'd pushed their control far enough. He repeated that refrain as he walked across the room and slid in next to her.

The mattress dipped. Before he could think it through, he rolled her to her side and wrapped a hand around her waist. Her back pressed against his chest, and his nose went into her hair. "You feel so good."

She brushed her hand across the arm banding her waist. "Go to sleep."

"I have to go out looking for Perry and Mark tomorrow."

She shifted until her hair hit the pillow and his body hovered over hers. "That's too dangerous."

"It's what I do."

She lifted a hand and skimmed her fingers over

his cheek. "You could wait for the rest of your team to arrive."

"Mark and Perry might need help and, if so, the clock would be ticking."

"But you think they're dead."

He hesitated, but her clear eyes had him telling the truth. "That's the worry, yes."

Thundered cracked in the distance and rain pounded the window. Being out in this would be rough on an experienced camper. He doubted two soft businessmen with little experience were faring all that well. Which left Joel with no choice— he had to get out there at sunup.

"I'm going with you."

"Not going to happen," he said in a scratchy voice.

The soft touch of her fingertips against his skin set off a fire inside him. He wanted her, would have been all over her, but he had promised. She'd set down the rules, and he intended to follow them. Even if it killed him, and he was starting to suspect it would.

She lifted her head and treated him to a lingering kiss before dropping back down again. "Then you really better sleep because tomorrow you'll have a fight on your hands."

The playful side of her…he loved this part. "Is that a threat?"

She winked and flipped over again, facing away from him. "You'll find out in a few hours."

Chapter Seven

The monster thunderstorm moved out, but the rain continued to fall in an annoying drizzle the next morning. The sky turned a hazy gray as the temperature held steady and the humidity rose. Dampness hung on the air and highlighted the smells of the forest. Fresh evergreen and the earthy scent of dirt and grass.

The scene felt familiar and, except for feeling sticky in her clothing, comfortable to Hope. She thrived in this environment. She also had packed the right gear. Sitting on the log turned into a makeshift seat, she wore a rain jacket and kept the hood up, ignoring the pings of raindrops against her face.

She would have stayed inside, where it was safer and certainly drier, and waited for the official breakfast hour to begin, but she had to deal with Joel. More like it, she had to deal with him being gone.

"There he is. Finally." Cam stood over her, staring into the mass of greenery off to the right of the cabins. "He's headed back in."

She could hear the relief in Cam's voice. The same feeling flooded through her. Joel had taken off, without a word to either of them, and headed out to sniper territory. In the world of dumb ideas, that one ranked pretty high up there.

"I should have known he'd skulk off." She blew out a long breath as the anxiety pinging around in her belly slowed. She stretched her legs out in front of her. "He's good at that."

"Not that I know anything about what happened between you two, because I don't." Cam sat down next to her and mimicked her position. "But he's not out in Annapolis partying with other women. I've never even see him checking out the ladies or making moves, and he's had opportunities."

That grumbly sensation came rushing back. "I bet."

"I'm just saying he attracts attention now and then, not that I'd ever admit that in front of him because I'm pretty invested in telling him how he lacks game."

She tried not to smile at that, at all of it. "Sure."

"At least now I know why he keeps the monk's existence."

That part made her beat back a dose of skepticism. Even when they were together she'd see women check him out and look for the chance to make a move. The fit body and hot smile combined with those dark looks and that bit of naughtiness in his eyes. Many women took a second look. He never noticed, that she could tell, but she'd assumed once he was free of their relationship he would. Just one more example of Joel reacting the opposite of how she thought he would.

"In some ways he's really complex—this mass of contradictions and frustrations—and in another he's transparent." Like the part where he ran scared from emotional entanglements. She was far too familiar with that side of him.

"His dad messed him up." Cam shook his head. "I never really saw how much before."

Her gaze snapped away from the man walking toward her and back to Cam. "He told you about his upbringing?"

"The end-of the-world fears imposed on him. The foster homes. Being separated from his sisters and never truly reconnecting with them again." Cam whistled. "Sometimes I'm amazed he can function, that he's as normal as he is. Don't tell him I admitted that either."

Joel's openness with Cam stunned her. Joel never hid his background or shied away from using his survival skills, but the idea of him talking it out with Cam was a surprise. She liked that Joel had someone close enough, and now she knew Cam wasn't just some random work friend.

But he'd used the magic word. The same one Joel loved to throw around. "That's the problem."

Cam frowned. "You lost me."

Through the dripping of the rain and soaking of the ground, Joel broke through the tree line. His footsteps hesitated for a second, and then he made a beeline for them.

She lowered her voice. "He thinks he can never be normal."

"Then he needs a good kick in the—"

"What are you two doing out here? You shouldn't be in the open." Joel stopped right by her feet. The scowl stayed as he scanned the area around them.

"We were waiting for you to wander back in," Cam said.

"I walked out a few hundred feet and did a perimeter check." Joel turned in a semicircle as his hand traced the trail through the air.

He acted like leaving was no big deal if he was the one doing it. He wasn't wearing a jacket and his shirt was soaked clear through. Never mind the fact there was some guy sitting out there waiting to shoot at them again. "Good thing a bullet can't reach that far."

"I was fine."

She rolled her eyes as she wondered how he would react if the roles were reversed. "This time."

Shuffling started behind her, then she heard

footsteps and the low mumble of male voices. Following Joel's gaze, she watched Lance and Jeff walk out to the fire pit area. Apparently no one wanted to stay inside where it was safer.

It wasn't exactly easy to take the two businessmen seriously with the drawstrings pulled tight on their hoods so only a fraction of their faces stood out. They acted as if acid fell from the sky.

She bit back a joke as she stood up, doubting Jeff would appreciate the humor. He'd dragged designer gear with him, most of which was more suitable for Himalayan climbing than camping in cabins.

Amateurs.

Joel nodded to the new members of the group. "Good morning."

"Where's Charlie?" she asked.

He popped up in the distance over Jeff's shoulder a second later carrying a steaming mug of something. "Breakfast is almost ready."

"Forget that." Jeff frowned at all of them. "What's the plan?"

Joel didn't move. "Survival."

One second he stood there alone. The next, Cam got up and took the place beside Joel. Together they formed a wall of lethal males.

Not that everyone got the message or understood the peril. Jeff sent Joel a withering look, one that probably worked when he tried intimidating his assistants. "I'm serious."

"So am I," Joel shot back.

Jeff dragged a foot through the mud before balancing it on the edge of the log. Never mind that people sat there. "Your timing is interesting."

Hope felt the conversation sliding sideways. Whatever point Jeff was trying to make had tension pounding harder than last night's thunder. He kept poking the bear and sooner or later, Joel would unleash. He had the skills to make Jeff look like an idiot, and she feared that showdown inched ever closer.

"What are you talking about?" Joel asked as he spread his stance and folded his arms behind him.

"You two show up and Mark disappears. Now you claim to have heard gunfire."

Joel's eyebrow lifted. "Claim?"

Enough testosterone-fueled nonsense. She stepped in. "It happened. I was there."

Jeff didn't even spare her a glance. "I'm just saying there are easier ways to get a woman into bed."

Joel took a threatening step forward. "That's enough." Only Cam's arm held him back.

"You're out of line, Jeff. Apologize," Charlie said at the same time.

But Jeff wasn't done. Clearly warming up to his theory, he stood taller and crossed his arms in front of him. "Maybe Mark snuck up on you? Maybe he was in the way? After all, the fight between Mark and Hope was explosive. Made me wonder if there was something behind all that anger."

She was two seconds from kicking the guy in the shin. "You should stop talking."

Joel nodded. "Listen to the lady."

Jeff threw his arms wide. "You going to make me?"

"Damn, you're stupid." Cam shook his head as he mumbled.

"Oh, really?"

Before Jeff could move, Charlie clamped a hand on his shoulder. "Sit."

Jeff shirked it off. "Why should I listen to you?"

"Because it's obvious Joel could take you out in a second, and I know the truth." Charlie took a long sip, drawing out the moment. "You and Mark had quite the argument after the gun incident."

Now, there was news that would have been helpful yesterday. Could have lessened some of her guilt, too. Confiscating the weapon had been the right answer, but doubts had bombarded her ever since. Maybe she could have been less firm about it or taken him aside. She'd always found that a show of strength cut down on some idiocy, but maybe she'd miscalculated this time.

"About what?" she asked, not trying to keep the seething anger out of her voice.

"Nothing you need to worry about." Jeff stepped back, separating himself from the group as he glanced around like a cornered animal. "This is insane. Charlie is just protecting her."

"My name is Hope." The guy was just not getting it. His coworkers were missing. This was not some game. "And what fight?"

Charlie shrugged. "I couldn't hear, but there was a lot of pushing and shouting."

Lance had stayed quiet, just watching and frowning. Now he moved, shoving a hand against Jeff's chest. "About what?"

"Don't touch me."

The more the minutes passed, the less Hope liked Jeff. He acted entitled and childish, and because neither Cam nor Joel looked ready to step in.

She did. "Boys, knock it off."

The shots rang out as she said the last word. Through the misty air and steady wind, the pings echoed.

"Everybody get down!" Joel yelled the order as he made a dive for Hope.

Lance beat him to it. He knocked into her stomach and they both went flying. She hit the ground hard, making a breath hiccup in her lungs. Knowing she had to move, she scrambled up and crawled on her knees and elbows to the log and tried to lie flat behind it.

Lance half covered her as he reached up and

tugged on Jeff's sleeve, breaking the spell that had frozen him in place and dragging him down in the mud beside them. Gunfire rang out. Glass shattered somewhere behind her and pieces of wood kicked up when a bullet slammed into the log right by her head.

She heard shouting and scuffling. The sharp smell of gunfire hit her, and a smoky haze filled the air.

Then Joel was there beside her. After a quick look up and down her torso, he and Cam crouched like a protective shield around the group. All but Charlie, who took off for the cabins behind them.

Noises blurred together and crescendoed to a rolling thunder. Everything seemed to rattle as her stomach rolled.

To steady her body, she reached forward and put her palm against the back of Joel's shirt. She wanted to pull him down and out of target range but settled for the touch. Anything to keep the contact.

In a blink it all stopped. No more loud banging and constant movements. Silence fell over them.

The wind blew and branches shifted. But the roar of noise that filled her ears ceased. Her hand clenched in Joel's shirt as the world came rushing back to her. She could make out Lance's heavy breathing as his weight fell against her. Jeff's whimpering sounded in the background. At least he'd stopped screaming his wife's name.

She heard the crunch of metal and looked behind her. Charlie stood on the cabin porch, half behind a post, with a shotgun in his hands. She had no idea where that had come from.

"Okay, let's double-time this before our friend comes back." Joel shifted around in his position, his gaze taking in the huddle of people behind him. "We need to get everyone inside."

Cam nodded as he came around the far end of the log and pulled Jeff to his feet. "Go right into Hope's cabin. Do not stop or hesitate."

An eerie quiet whispered through the trees. It made her want to bolt for the indoors. Sitting up proved impossible with Lance pinning her leg to the ground.

"We need to go." She pushed against his shoulder, trying to get him to pull out of his ducking position, but he didn't move. "It's okay now. You can move."

Joel stood watch. "Cam, get them inside now."

A new sensation stabbed at her. One of pure panic. The type that had something twisting in her gut. "Lance?"

The tone must have caught Joel's attention because his sweeping gaze landed on her. "What's wrong?"

She put a hand on Lance's shoulder and shook. Still nothing. Pulling it back, she saw the red.

The color drained right out of her as she looked up at Joel. "Blood."

TONY HADN'T ENJOYED his first conversation with Connor Bowen and didn't relish a second one. From the time the man left the office yesterday until this morning, Tony had conducted an impromptu investigation.

It paid to know the man on the other side of the conference room table and be ready for anything. Tony always was, but he hadn't counted on this guy. He expected Hope to be connected, thanks to her father, but word was her life focused on climbing and, now that she'd messed up that career, she was floundering.

That had proved to be only part of the story. Looked like she knew powerful men in dangerous places. Men who didn't know when to back off.

Connor and his team worked in the intelligence field, and his record possessed the shiny, perfect look that came with false IDs. Tony would bet they dealt in hush-hush projects. That made Connor and anyone who worked for him a huge liability.

Tony stared at his closed office door and reasoned out his next steps. He'd worked too long and too hard to get to this uncertain place.

He'd earned his reputation for being ruthless the honest way. He'd move into a company and cut staff and streamline costs and personnel, rarely getting the credit he deserved. The career had him relocating and trading positions while trying to make a series of corporate boards happy.

But this position was his ticket. Show the right numbers and growth, and the big desk would stay his. He would be in charge and the impressive paycheck and windfall bonuses would come his way.

With one sharp knock, his office door opened. So much for his crack staff and the security measures he'd put in place to keep anyone from getting into his office without permission. Connor somehow broke through the protocol after one visit to the place.

That meant one thing: Tony had to get the pseudo-detective out of his business and off his trail. Fast.

He didn't give Connor the satisfaction of mentioning the unapproved entrance. "You're back."

Connor didn't bother with small talk. He walked right across the large office to stand in front of Tony's desk. "I have a few questions."

Not that Tony had any intention of answering them. "Where's your assistant?"

"Second in command."

He leaned back in his chair and slid his palms

over the smooth leather of the armrests. "Is there a difference?"

Connor took a quick look around the office. His gaze roamed but he didn't move. "Davis is back at the office, working on this case."

"Case?"

"Yes."

"Exactly how long are you in town?" The man needed to head back to Annapolis and stay there. Tony was half ready to throw him in a cab to make it happen.

"For as long as it takes."

"Interesting response."

Connor's stance relaxed from attack mode to soon-to-attack. The dark suit didn't fool Tony. He knew a fellow fighter when he saw one. This man could ruin everything. He would dig and push, and those were the two things Tony could not afford to have happen.

Without being asked, Connor launched into whatever he came to say. "I thought you could give me some intel on your officers."

The man had guts. Tony had to give him that, but the request, if that's what it was, would never happen. "Intel?"

"Who, what, backgrounds. Personality types." Other than blinking, Connor still didn't move. "Likelihood for trouble."

Tony tapped his fingers against the end of

the armrest. He aimed for mild disinterest. Inside his mind was spinning with ways to end the conversation. "This is starting to sound a bit like an interrogation."

"If it helps you to think of it that way, I'm good with that." The flat tone only added to the feeling of menace.

"It's also a clear case of overreaching."

"Your executive *is* missing."

And what a mess that had turned out to be. "I let you get me upset last time, but this is nothing. Mark wandered away from camp. That's hardly a reason to dig around in people's personal lives."

Connor's eyes narrowed a fraction. "Why do you say that?"

"Because it's not your business where they—"

"I meant the part about Mark. Why do you think he walked off?"

"It's the most logical explanation." That was the story. That was the plan. Simple and straightforward. Except for the part where it all blew apart and now Tony had to deal with bad weather, Rafe screaming on the phone from thousands of miles away about his baby girl's safety and the man across the desk who wanted to rush in and save everyone.

"I told you there were gunshots."

"I doubt it," Tony said. "If that were true, if there were really trouble, the police, park rangers and everyone else would be out there. I'd be getting calls and this would be on the news. You see, Mr. Bowen—"

"Connor is fine."

"Conner then." Though Tony would prefer not to get so personal. "I turned this company around by being patient. I don't run off or act in panic mode."

"You think I do?"

"Technically, isn't other people's panic your business?" Tony continued to drum his fingers. With each tap he inhaled, trying to slow down his pounding heart and keep his breathing under control. There was no need to show weakness. "Look, Mark likes to show off. He wasn't thrilled with the idea of a young woman running the retreat."

"How evolved of him."

Little did Connor know the woman, Hope, had been a vital part of the plan. Talk about a miscalculation. "My guess is his male ego got wounded and now he's stuck trying to find a reasonable way to save face and come back to camp."

"Is that it?"

"Excuse me?"

"Are you done?" This time Connor moved. He leaned forward with his fists on the far edge of Tony's desk and kept the eye contact locked on him. "If so, let me tell you about my men. They don't panic. They also know what gunfire sounds like because they're experts at rescuing. When they issue a warning it's because something is seriously wrong."

"So you're impressed with your men." By the time he finished, the words rang out in the room. It took all of Tony's control to keep his expression blank and not shift in his chair. "Your point is?"

Connor pushed up and stood straight again. "I take off as soon as the weather clears."

"This is a waste of time and money."

"Possibly, but it's my time and my money to waste."

"Not really since it's my men out there on the retreat." Tony needed to bring them in clean and without them being subjected to questioning. Not unless he could control it, and he knew Connor wouldn't let that happen "My suggestion would be to let this play out. I paid for a certain number of days and want those men out there, including Mark, who will show up soon, in the woods, building rapport as promised."

"While getting shot at."

"I think we've discussed that issue enough." Until Tony knew more about the who and why of the gunshots, he pivoted around the topic.

"I agree."

Forget relief. Anxiety smacked into him. "You're still going."

"I'm getting my people out."

That superman complex was going to ruin everything. Tony sensed it. "I guess that's your choice."

Connor nodded. "I'll let you know what Mark says."

"Meaning?"

"When I find him, I'll get him to talk. Because, *Tony,* I will find him. That's what I do."

Chapter Eight

Hope stood behind Cam and looked out the small window next to her cabin door. The rainy gray sky beyond didn't provide much light, so they had to rely on a few dull bulbs.

The small space was lined wall to wall with mud-soaked men. The mixed scent of wet clothes and stale air in the confined room gave it the feel of a locker room, though he'd smelled worse, but for her this couldn't be good.

After the frantic racing around outside and piling inside the cabin, Joel could finally breathe. Hearing the familiar crack and watching Hope fall had taken a good twenty years off his life. When she'd moved and Lance had covered her, Joel forced his mind on the attacker, but the twisting-gut fear about her getting hurt had kept him off his game.

Somehow they'd made it with minimal injuries. Hers being the biggest cabin and having the only indoor shower, it won as the staging area—

a good place to regroup and plan. And in Lance's case, receive medical treatment.

Charlie was in the other room now while Jeff paced outside the door. Joel had ordered they all rotate in the bathroom and then put on dry clothes. He had enough to worry about without having someone get deathly ill, and he was willing to do anything to keep Jeff occupied. The man was walking around in circles mumbling about finding a new job.

Now Joel hovered over Lance where he sat on the arm of the couch. The stitching would have been done five minutes ago if the guy would stop jerking and hissing. You'd think he'd never been injured before.

Sure, the shot was a bit more than a flesh wound, but not much more. They all had scrapes and bruises, but Lance delivered most of the flinching. How he'd ever made it through his wife giving birth was a mystery.

With one last stitch, Joel dropped a bloody bandage in the small trash can by his feet. He kept up a running dialogue with Lance, thinking it might calm the man down. "You got lucky."

Lance winced as Joel wrapped a clean bandage around his upper arm. "We might have different definitions of that word."

"I'm not even going to mention that you passed

out from a puny shot in the arm." Okay, maybe he'd mention it that one time, but now he'd stop.

"I thought I was dead."

Joel had worried a bullet hit Hope, and the punch of pain had nearly knocked him over. Although he didn't want anyone hurt, he wasn't upset Lance had caught it instead.

He was about to thank him for trying to protect Hope, but she broke in. "There isn't a special prize for the least amount of tears when shot."

"I didn't cry." Lance's voice rose as if swearing under his breath didn't telegraph his disgust for the suggestion.

"Because you were unconscious," Cam said without ending his surveillance on the world outside the cabin.

Joel chuckled. He could go a lifetime without seeing whiny Jeff again, but Joel liked Lance. Charlie, now, he was an enigma. Joel had no idea what to think about that guy.

When Lance glanced down at the white bandage and the line of red seeping through, the color left his face. Joel rushed to reassure him. It was either that or risk having the guy pass out again. "The bullet went through and didn't knick anything important."

"It hurts like a—"

"I have some painkillers," Hope broke in as she

left her position by the window and squatted down to drag a bag out from under the bed.

"That would be good." Joel pointed at Jeff. "You're next."

The guy stopped mid-pace. "I wasn't hit."

"I meant answers."

Hope frowned at Joel. Took a second and shot most of the men in the room a frown, even Cam, and he wasn't looking at her. "Now might not be the time for a chat."

This topic was not up for debate. Joel's patience had expired. So had his willingness to sit around and wait to become a target. "Someone is shooting at us and we have two unskilled men missing in this miserable weather. So if Jeff here knows something, it's time to speak up."

"I don't."

Hope got to her feet and grabbed a water bottle on her way over to Lance. Her gaze never left Jeff. "Why did you fight with Mark?"

"It has nothing to do with..." Jeff exhaled as he ran a hand through his wet hair. "Look, it was a work issue."

That got Lance's attention. "What was it?"

Whatever Jeff heard in Lance's voice or saw on his face had his shoulders slumping. "He had these private meetings with Tony—"

"Who?" Cam asked.

"Tony Prather, Baxter's CEO." Jeff kept up the

steady stream of sighing. "It felt like Mark was making a play. Going around my back."

"Doesn't Mark rank above you in the corporate scheme?" Hope asked. "He's the vice president, not you."

Leave it to her to point that out. Joel wished he had. "Exactly my question. Jeff?"

"I had some ideas about positioning the company moving forward. One of the divisions had a down quarter but seemed to be bouncing back, and I wanted to capitalize on the upswing." Jeff leaned against the wall and let his head fall back. "I give Mark some notes, he studies them and all of a sudden he's having private meetings with our boss."

Joel could see it all playing out. Jeff, with his oversized ego, wouldn't accept being pushed out. He'd want every ounce of credit he could squeeze out of an idea. "That ticked you off."

Jeff looked around the room. "Wouldn't it do the same to you?"

"Don't know since I've never worked in an office," Cam said.

Joel reached into the specialized first aid kit for another bandage roll as he turned over Jeff's comments in his mind. The man had just handed them a motive. Not a compelling reason to kill in Joel's view, but for Jeff's type it could be. Always looking for an angle, expecting to rise in the ranks at record speed, wanting the perks and big title. Watching someone grab that away could be a brutal ego blow for someone like Jeff.

Reading people was not his strength. Joel glanced at Hope, looking for her take on the situation. She had good instincts. But because she stood right at Cam's shoulder, looking out the window instead of at Jeff, Joel couldn't tell what she was thinking.

Now Joel wanted to know what had caught her attention and held it so long. "Cam, can you take over for a second?"

"Sure."

The men passed each other in the middle of the room, exchanging gun for bandage. By the time Joel got to the window, Hope stood right in front of it. Talk about becoming a target. With her damp, freshly showered hair pulled in a ponytail and clean white shirt, she stuck out among the group.

Without making a big deal of it, he shifted her out of the direct firing line through the window and lowered his voice. "You okay?"

"You're very handy with a first aid kit."

He noticed she skipped his question, but he decided to let it slide. "One of the many skills demanded by my father."

"He brought about so much bad, but every now and then there's something positive."

"I think you're reaching for a silver lining."

Joel remembered every minute of the last day as a family—protective services ripping his sisters away, the standoff with the police, the shot his dad fired that finally landed him in jail—so he knew the truth. Nothing good happened. Joel couldn't point to one decent thing about the way he grew up either before or after the final takedown of the Kidd family.

She bit her lower lip. "I keep hoping to find something positive about your upbringing."

"That's not an easy task."

She clearly tried to get it. She listened and shook her head at all the right places.

The pain in her eyes as he relayed the facts, some of them anyway, was genuine. It bordered on pity, and Joel hated that. Knew it was human nature but still despised it. Connor and Cam and the few other people in his life who knew bits and pieces also tried to reason it out, but Joel knew that without living it you could never really understand.

Hope had grown up in a loving home with a father who doted on her. Not every day was easy, of course. She'd lost her mother to cancer when she was a young girl, but Hope never worried about having food or running a drill about how to escape the police. She loved her dad. Joel had seen the bond. It bordered on overprotective, but it beat strong.

"I assure you that if Dad had known I would use my abilities to work for any government agency or a team that helps governments, he likely would have shot me on the spot." That was the threat— *disappoint me and you're dead.*

Hope froze. "Why do I think you're not kidding?"

"If only." She'd moved in closer, which put her head back in the line of fire, so he shifted her to the side again. "You need to stand away from the window."

She looked at him and then to that spot outside that seemed to capture her attention. Through the driving rain and storm that had whipped up right when it looked as if it would taper off, she'd focused in on that area.

"What is it?" he asked.

"You know about trajectories, right?"

If this had anything to do with his dad, Joel lost the track on how. "Sure."

"One of the ways I perfected my aim in archery was to track the trajectory of my arrow. First I played with my stance and did all this math to figure out the proper draw length, and then I got this fancy computer program. Point is, I figured out I was starting out too high and then the drop off…" She smiled. "You should see your face."

"You have to admit this is an odd conversation in light of being trapped in a cabin and all." He put his body in front of her and brought up the binoculars to scan the area.

"True, but the bottom line is Lance's entry wound is higher than the exit." She drew a diagram in the condensation on the window. "I felt Lance get shot. We were on the ground and the bullet came from above, so the angle isn't a surprise, but it's off."

Something had clicked together in her mind. He could see the light go on and hear the growing excitement in her voice. The energy bouncing off her was contagious.

But he still wasn't sure about her point. "That leads you to believe what?"

"I think the shots came not just from someone standing above Lance but from someone in the trees. The trajectory is that steep."

The comment hung there. Even Cam looked up from finishing off Lance's arm. Jeff was the only one who'd missed the discussion. He was too busy trading places with Charlie as he came out of the bathroom in a set of clean clothes that looked exactly like the dirty ones he had just shed.

Hope's intelligence focused all the pieces. As usual, she found a way through the confusion and came up with a reasonable explanation. She was smart and sharp and didn't hide it.

He loved that about her. Of course, he loved pretty much everything about her.

Still, he wanted to make sure they were on the same page. "So you're saying this guy is sitting up in a branch shooting?"

"I think it's a good possibility the shots came from there, but that doesn't answer every question."

"Okay."

"If I'm right about the position, the shooter should have been able to pick us off one by one because we were all truly vulnerable." She stabbed her finger against points in the diagram on the glass. "That leaves us with a bigger problem."

That's what they needed. More problems. "Which is?"

"Neither Perry nor Mark is the athletic scaling-trees type."

Joel hadn't met either man, but he totally trusted her view on this. He could climb and she could probably do it faster than he could, and that was saying something. That didn't mean two businessmen who spent most of their time sitting behind desks had a chance at getting up there. There was a slight possibility that one of them, or one of the men in the cabin, pretended to be clueless and really had sniper tree-climbing skills, but Joel doubted it.

"We're talking some random guy out here

shooting for fun." Joel glanced at Cam. His grim expression mirrored Joel's thoughts—that was the absolute worst case scenario. A pure risk and someone they couldn't get a handle on.

Lance made a strangled sound but didn't say anything.

"Unfortunately, the theory leads to more questions. I mean, how would the random guy get down without you or Cam seeing him?" She pointed to the open space outside as she asked.

Joel had that exact question. There were possible explanations, but none of them proved all that convincing. Cam and Joel were trained. They were on high alert. Even as worrying about Hope getting hurt occupied part of Joel's mind, Cam stayed fully focused.

"It was raining and we were being shot at," Cam said from across the room.

"And you stood out there like a human shield." Hope stopped whispering and went back to her normal voice. "All I'm saying is if someone wanted to kill you, someone with the level of skill to balance in a tree with a gun and then sneak away unseen by two covert agents, he would have killed you."

Charlie stopped running the towel over his wet hair. "What are you guys talking about?"

Hope ignored the older man and talked to Joel. "All the advantage goes to the person in that position. If that were you, you'd hit the target without trouble."

"So would you." Joel knew that was true because she was the most competent woman he'd ever met.

"Where does that leave us?" Cam asked.

Joel fought the temptation to handle the issue now. He just needed the weather to give him a five-minute shot at testing her theory. "With lots of questions and something to do as soon as the storm breaks."

Her eyes narrowed. "Which is?"

"Go out there and look around."

Two hours later the rain had morphed into a steady fall, but the dark sky gave way to white and the wind died down. While Charlie watched from the porch with a gun in his hand, Hope ventured outside with Cam and Joel.

They fought to have her stay behind, but she refused. Because she threatened to follow them the minute they stepped outside, they gave in and brought her along.

They trudged along on either side of her until they walked a few feet into the wooded area and well within shouting distance of the cabins. Both men had guns and she carried the binoculars but had a gun and her knife within grabbing range.

Cam shifted into the lead as they got close to

the tree they'd staked out as the best contender for climbing. "Remind me again why we're doing this?"

"A hunch." That's all she had, but she'd calculated all the angles and run through all the alternatives, and this was the only one that made sense.

"Seems like a dangerous hunch."

"Not if Hope is right." They stopped at the tree and Joel tapped his palm against the bark.

"Which is why I get to be out here, too." No matter what they thought, she didn't plan to stand around and watch. "I'll climb."

Joel snorted. "No way."

"You two are better to guard and I can—"

Joel broke her concentration when he snatched the binoculars and flung them around his neck. Next came the standing jump where he grabbed the lowest branch, which wasn't all that low. The move stretched him out and had his T-shirt riding up and showing off his flat stomach. With an impressive pull-up, he was up and gone in a matter of seconds, leaving her sputtering.

Cam laughed. "He's fast when he wants to be. He's also smart enough to know you're likely better at that than he is and he had to beat you to the punch."

Joel's voice reached them from above. "Maybe less talking since we could be wrong about this and have a guy stalking us even now."

That reality check had her back teeth knocking together. She'd pushed the fear out, insisting she could handle this…somehow.

With that warning, Cam backed her up against the tree and put his body in front of hers until no part of her was exposed. The bulletproof vest Joel made her wear before he opened the cabin door gave her added protection.

If someone came shooting, Cam would go down and she'd have a shot. The mere idea of that had her stomach flipping around.

She cleared her voice and looked up. Beads of rain fell, hitting her face and running under her hood and into her hair. "See anything?"

From this position she spied a flash of blue jeans and the bottom of Joel's hiking boots. His voice sounded distant and the rain muffled every sound.

"It would help if it stopped pouring." That grumble came through loud and clear.

Cam kept watch as his back pressed into her chest. "Take that up with another department."

Joel shifted and she could make him out as he balanced on a branch. He faced deeper into the woods.

She pushed the panic out of her mind. Others might wobble or slide off. Not Joel. He could probably live up there if he had to.

His arms went up and she knew he was taking a look around. "I want a pair of those binoculars."

"We'll get you a pair," Cam said.

"Hold on," Joel called out.

"What?" She looked up and Cam joined her.

"There's something in the trees about thirty feet out."

Hope's body threatened to break into a full shake. She clenched her hands into fists to keep from fidgeting and shifting around. "A person?"

"A rigging of some kind."

She shook her head as the constant thudding of rain against her jacket had her talking louder. "I don't even know what that means."

"A platform and a gun set-up to fire either at specific times or via remote." Cam spared her a quick look before he went back to checking out the area around them. "A human might not be pulling the trigger now, but a human built the rigging."

"So we're back to everyone being a suspect." She didn't know if that was good or bad. With the businessmen as suspects she at least knew something about her potential attacker.

A rogue sniper terrified her. That suggested someone with skill and put Joel and Cam at greater risk because she knew they would shield the rest of them with their bodies if it came to that.

The thought of watching Joel go down almost drove her to her knees.

"Move." A loud whoosh followed the warning. Joel shouted as he dropped out of the branches and landed with a slight bend of his knees as if he'd been practicing the move his entire life.

She heard a thud and saw the binoculars land in the mud. Adrenaline pumped through her as she spun around, looking for the danger that had set him off.

The forest blurred in front of her. Joel grabbed Cam's shoulder and turned him toward the cabins while Joel shoved her behind him and brought up his gun. The men took up positions behind two trunks and faced in the same direction, this time toward camp.

Despite the dizzying few seconds, she stayed locked behind Joel with her fingers slipped through his belt loop.

"Hands up," Joel yelled in the direction off to the side of the far cabin.

She peeked around his shoulder and saw trees and branches and sheets of water. Nothing moved and no sound came. She was about to ask what was happening when a smaller tree bent. The wind didn't take this one. A shadow moved.

"Come out or we fire." Joel pushed her deeper behind the tree as he motioned for Cam to take the far side. "You have three seconds."

She shifted and looked out from the other side of the tree. Then she saw it. The shadow, clearly a large figure, stumbled. "Joel, I think—"

"One…"

"An animal maybe?" Cam asked.

"Two."

Without a sound, the figure dropped. A man's torso fell into the clearing with the rest left behind in the woods. Arms outstretched and a familiar green polo shirt. The rain pounded his face, which was turned toward them.

She started to rush out, but Joel caught her arm. "Wait."

Cam's shoulders fell as he lowered the weapon. "What the—"

But she knew exactly who it was. "It's Perry."

Chapter Nine

They'd informally shared her town house and slept together more times than he could count, but when he stepped into Hope's confining cabin that night he still felt about three sizes too big. "At least it smells better in here than it did ten minutes ago."

She glanced over at him and smiled. "Who knew a candle could help that much?"

The men had cleared out, with Charlie taking the cabin on one side of hers and dragging Lance and Jeff along with him. Cam was looking after their newest patient, Perry, next door while keeping the first watch on the camp.

The man hadn't roused long enough to answer even one question. The nasty gash on the back of his head suggested a fall or a hit. Joel was betting on the latter.

They had gotten it bandaged, and Cam had agreed to wake him up in a few hours for a concussion check. Other than that, all they knew was

Perry had the same clothes on when he stumbled back into camp that he had worn the night of Mark's fight with Hope.

Every time Joel started to think they'd all walked into some big work argument between Perry and Mark, the reality of that gun rigging would strike. Joel just couldn't see either man having the skills for that, never mind the equipment. Hope said she had done a bag check…of course, Mark got a gun through, so maybe it wasn't impossible.

Joel took one last sweeping look out the door, then shut it behind him. The rain still fell, but the wind no longer whipped through the trees. He toyed with the idea of loading everyone up and heading for the helicopter, but the darkness and memory of the uneven ground stopped him. Last thing they needed was another injury.

"Still nothing from Perry?" She wadded the old sheet and blanket into a ball and threw them on the floor.

"He's out cold." Trying hard not to think of the bed and her in it, and failing miserably, Joel walked to the farthest point from her.

He should help her strip and remake the bed after they'd laid Perry out there. His clothes had been caked with mud and his shirt soaked with blood. But that side of the room spelled trouble. Even with the danger spinning around them, Joel wanted her and his self-control was going down for the count.

She froze in the act of unzipping her sleeping bag and spreading it over the bare mattress. "Any chance we could lose him during the night?"

Joel decided to go with the least panicked version. "Cam is staying with Perry. We're worried about a concussion. His head is pretty banged up."

"Maybe he got lost and the exposure—"

"No." Joel couldn't let her think that. Not when he needed her on guard for the worst-case scenario. "Something slammed into his head. Either he fell or he got hit."

Her expression hardened. "Where's Jeff right now?"

"Jeff, Charlie and Lance are bunking together." Joel understood her narrow-eyed reaction because he also had suspicions about Jeff. Though the evidence pointed toward Mark as the attacker, something wasn't right with Jeff. Something Joel couldn't nail down. "I want someone with weapons knowledge in each cabin. I don't know if I can trust Charlie, but I trust him more than Jeff."

She dropped onto the bed and balanced a hand on the mattress on either side of her trim hips. "When can we leave?"

This he could handle. Simple emotionless conversation. Joel didn't like the idea of Lance and Perry being hurt or Mark being on the loose, but getting them out of there alive gave Joel something to concentrate on…instead of thinking about her. "I'm not sure if we can move Perry. Without medical help, I can't really assess how bad off he is, and I don't want to drag him around and cause more damage."

"So we're going to live here now?"

"Hardly." Joel bit back the wave of heat hitting him. She sat there in thin sweats and an even thinner tee, looking vulnerable, and his mind started flipping back to them as a couple. He cleared his throat and forced his mind to clear. "A group will go to the helicopter. If we can rig some sort of gurney, we may be able to carry Perry out and all go to the clearing."

She frowned. "With a sniper out there?"

"First thing tomorrow I'll check that station in the tree. I'm guessing I'll find a jerry-rigged weapon and no space for a human shooter." He sure hoped that was the case.

The scenario would at least give them a direction. Someone on foot with a gun could easily pick them off one by one as they lumbered along dragging Perry on a slab.

There was a nightmare thought. A rigged gun had a limited attack range. A human on foot spelled real danger.

"And that means we can walk through the

woods." She rubbed her hands together until the skin turned red.

"I think we need to take the risk." He walked over and sat next to her. "Speaking of which, you were pretty impressive today."

"I got lucky."

He slipped his hand over hers and stopped her fidgeting before she rubbed her skin raw. "I'm thinking your climbing skills and all those years of archery helped."

"I'll give you the archery."

"Not the climbing?"

She shrugged. "I stick with normal climbing now."

"Why?" He knew the story because he'd never stopped watching over her, making sure she was okay.

Part of the story anyway. He could tell from the nervous energy that she kept part of it trapped inside her and it needed to come out.

"A burst of sanity?"

His thumb rubbed over the back of her hand, and his thigh touched hers. "Hope, this is me. I know how much you love climbing. I've been along with you, seen your face."

"To be fair, I'm a fan of almost anything that happens outside."

He wasn't buying it, refused to let her dismiss

this. "You excelled at taking groups up. Your dad didn't like it, but it was a good living."

"Until it wasn't."

The monotone voice tugged at him. "What piece am I missing?"

"The accident." Her free hand brushed over their joined ones. "Come on, you talk with my dad, right? You know about this."

Joel had read the news articles about it and gotten the basic information from her dad. Joel knew it was a horrible accident—not her fault—but it didn't sound like she did. "I know you took a group up Mt. Rainier and bad weather rolled in."

She sighed and her shoulders fell. "Two men died, Joel."

"You're not responsible for an unexpected snowstorm, Hope."

"But I am the one responsible for knowing when to turn around." She loosened her grip on his hand.

"Wait a minute." He held on, even squeezed her palm until she looked at him again. "I read the file—"

"What are you talking about?"

He refused to be derailed by the rising anger in her voice. "You've tracked me, at least a little, because you know I live in Annapolis. Well, I know what you've been doing since we broke up, and the point is you trained that group and when something happened, a guy panicked and took his friend down the mountain with him."

"We should have—"

"The other people in the group said you insisted everyone go down. You followed your own rules and didn't screw around. The guy ignored you."

"It was as if he expected me to chase him up the mountain."

"Not to speak ill of the dead, but his ego took over. That's on him, not you." Joel had watched her struggle with male stupidity more than once in her work. She had all the skills and knowledge, but you put a bunch of guys together and sometimes a certain type would show off. Add in how pretty she was and some guys underestimated her.

Joel never did. She was stunning and fierce… and he loved her as much today as he did when he had walked out. Maybe more.

"All he had to do was turn around and slam his ax into the ice." She whispered the words, lost in whatever mental image played in her head. "He was tied to his friend and they both raced down the slope and…"

"Listen to me." Joel's hand went into her hair and he turned her to face him. "I deal with danger and guilt all the time. I know the difference between negligence and horrible tragedy. You lived through the latter."

"It destroyed my love of climbing."

He leaned in and kissed her because he couldn't stand not to right then. "It's too soon to know that."

"I just wanted to start over, find something else I loved, and now this." She tucked her head under his chin.

"Also not your fault."

The vanilla scent of her shampoo and smell of her skin had his mind blanking. He had to close his eyes to stay in comfort mode and away from whatever mode it was that had him wanting to push her back into the sleeping bag.

"The comment is funny coming from you." Her hand pressed against his chest, and her fingers toyed with the neck band of his T-shirt. "You take on the weight of everyone else's sins and let them define your life."

"That's not true." He wouldn't let that be true.

She lifted her head then and stared at him with those big brown eyes. "You left me because of things that have nothing to do with us."

She kissed his chin. Let her fingertips dance over his cheek.

"Hope, don't—"

"You love me." She pressed her fingers to his lips.

He kissed the tips. "Always."

"Yet we're not together."

"My feelings and reality are two different

things." The mantra played in his head, but his body and his heart rebelled. The need for her kicked strong enough to knock him over.

Being this close to her, holding her, seemed so easy. Made him doubt everything he believed about how his life should go. How he should stay alone rather than risk dragging someone else into his life.

Bottom line was he could easily become his father one day. The old man had been normal once, or so their old neighbors said. But at some point, he'd lost it. Joel worried every day he'd travel down the same road.

No, he was right. They couldn't make this work. "We're never going to agree on this."

"How about this?" She swept her lips over his, gentle and quick.

His temperature spiked and somewhere in his brain an alarm bell rang. "What are you doing?"

"Wow, it really has been a long time for you, hasn't it?" Her sexy smile promised a sleepless night.

It also smashed through his control with the destructive crush of a bulldozer. "This is a bad idea."

"Then let's do something bad." She slid out of his arms and fell back against the mattress with her hair spilling over the small pillow.

Maybe if he kept saying her name his brain would have time to restart. "Hope…"

Having none of it, she pulled him down on top of her. "You want me. I want you."

He balanced his weight on his elbows and stared down at her. "What we feel is deeper than that, and sleeping together could mess it all up."

It took every last bit of his strength to get the words out. He didn't mean them and hated saying them.

Her arms wrapped around his neck, and her body slid against his. "Do you honestly think our relationship could be a bigger mess than it is?"

"We broke up." But he had nothing left. No way to fight her.

"And neither of us has moved on." She treated him to a lingering kiss. "Do you want me to move on, Joel?"

Hell, no. "You need—"

"You."

The next kiss didn't brush or linger. It burned. Her tongue touched his and her hot mouth had him reeling.

When he lifted his head again he could barely breathe and his brain stuck on permanent misfire. "I have exactly one condom."

Her eyebrow lifted. "I'm a little surprised you have even that."

"Call it wishful thinking, but when I knew I was coming to you—"

"Go get it." She whispered the command against his mouth.

He scrambled out of the bed and grabbed the wallet out of his pocket. After a second, he dropped it on the floor.

Before he could climb back onto the bed, she was there, sitting on the edge. Her fingers went to work on his belt, then his zipper. The screech echoed through the quiet room as she lowered it.

Her hand covered him and her breath blew across his boxer briefs. Looking down and seeing her hair, feeling her soft hand on his erection, proved to be too much. The last of his common sense fled as he threw the condom on the bed and pushed her back.

Hands roamed everywhere. His, hers, it didn't matter. His shirt came off and then hers. It wasn't until he saw her bare skin and the sweet shadow between her breasts that he forced his body to slow down, to savor.

He skimmed his fingers over the smooth skin of the top of her breasts, then slipped a finger inside the edge of a plain white bra. At that moment, the sexiest bra he'd ever seen. With a teasing flick over her nipple through the material, he heard her gasp.

"I can't forget you." His mouth went to her neck as he said the startling truth in a gruff voice.

"Don't."

He felt the tug of his pants and felt them slide down farther on his hips, freeing him. Her hand slipped past the elastic band of his underwear and then she was on him, skin against skin, and he had to grind his back teeth together from ending this too soon.

"I want you." He told her right before he kissed her, not giving him a chance to take it back or her a chance to question.

His lips crossed over hers as the heat rolled through him. A signal went off in his brain. Protection…it was there somewhere. His hand patted the bed, searching for the condom. Adrenaline pounded him and he was about to rip the sleeping bag apart to find it when she picked it up and held it in front of his face.

"Looking for this?"

He didn't say anything. Couldn't. He plucked it out of her hand and tore through the paper. His body was on fire now. He had to have her, to sink into her again.

Desperate to make it good for her, he ran a hand over her stomach and hit the band of her pants. Yeah, those had to come off. He didn't waste a second as he stripped them down, taking her bikini bottoms with them and throwing the rumpled ball to the floor.

Then she was naked and open, her legs falling to the side to make room for him between them.

When he dragged a finger through her heat, her back arched off the bed.

She was wet and ready. She didn't pretend shyness. He could read the need on her face and see the excitement in the pink hue of her skin.

It was all the invitation he needed. Rolling the condom on, he fit his tip to her and pushed. His body plunged into hers as it always had, with a tightness that made a groan rumble up the back of his throat.

The night fell away and the closeness of the other cabins didn't matter. He was back inside her as he'd fantasized about for so long. And he wanted it to last. He stilled, enjoying the feel of her tight body around his.

She pinched his shoulder. "Joel, move."

But his body had already taken over. He pressed in and pulled back out. A steady rhythm gave way to a frantic beating of his blood. Her nails dug into his shoulder as she whispered his name in his ear.

He kissed her, touched her, made love to her as the driving need took over. Tension coiled inside him. The building started in every limb. That's what she did to him. Destroyed his intentions and stole control over his body.

Unable to hold back, he slid a hand between them and touched her. A slight circle with his finger and her head pressed back. When her mouth dropped open he covered it with his, thinking to catch those delicious gasps he loved so much as she found her release.

The orgasm slammed into him a second later. His body let go and his shoulders shook until he thought they wouldn't hold him. With one last push, he surrendered.

His last thought was that he hadn't taken the time to pull his pants off.

Chapter Ten

An alarm buzzed beside her head, breaking into Hope's delicious dream. She thought about throwing it at the wall.

When her eyes opened and she adjusted to the overhead light and darkness outside the window, it all came rushing back. Joel's arm across her stomach. His breath against her neck. The memories of the kissing and touching. Making love with him, feeling him over her. Rolling around after and his cursing once he remembered they only had one condom.

She'd wanted another morning after with him for so long. It was somewhere around three and not yet sunrise, but this was close enough.

Through the waves of anger and hurt all those months ago and every day since, she knew they'd get back to this emotional place. That they weren't over. The real question was how long they could stay in this holding position.

The temptation to hide under the blanket and

forget the world and the horrors outside the cabin rushed over her. She hated to wake him, but that was the deal. One person on guard duty, and Cam had been handling that for hours.

Now, deep into the night, rain still pinged against the cabin and the alarm on his simple black watched sounded a second time. No question about it, it was Joel's turn to stand guard.

"I want to stay in bed with you." Joel mumbled the comment into her hair.

She had to smile at the grumbling. "Cam would kill you."

The man protected for a living and could shoot anything, track anything, catch anything, yet he hated waking up. It had always been that way with Joel. Morning came and he whined and groaned and tried to get her to stay in bed beside him.

He'd concoct elaborate scenarios just to win another ten minutes. When that failed, he'd start kissing her, and he'd always won the bed battle once that happened.

"Trust me, Cam would understand." Joel lifted up and balanced over her on one elbow. "He can't believe I let you get away the first time."

"Me either."

She hadn't said the words last night because she wanted him to accept the risk and tell her first, but she did love him. They'd said it before and it didn't stop him from walking out. She had no idea if it would matter now. The not knowing made her want to knock some sense into him.

His mouth opened, then closed. It took another few seconds before he said anything. "I walked into that one."

"And, technically, you left me."

He groaned and sat up. "On that note, I'll get out of bed now."

Naked and not even a little shy about it, he threw his feet over the side of the bed. He wiped his face with his open hand but didn't cover his body. Just looked around the floor.

"I'm going to regret this a few hours from now when I'm trudging through the forest dead on my feet," she said as she gathered the lone blanket against her bare skin and sat up. "Now I just have to find my clothes."

He glanced over his shoulder at her. "What are you doing?"

"Coming with you."

This time he stood up. "You are not."

Her body flushed at the sight of him. He was long and fit, and the idea of crawling back into bed and pulling him in there with her nearly won out. But they needed to keep moving and get ready to head out.

She had no idea what would happen between them back in the real world, but she knew she'd be safer there. "I'm not staying in this cabin alone."

"I will be right outside. Guard duty consists of sitting on the porch with a gun and shooting anything or anyone I don't recognize."

She spied his pants at the end of the bed, underwear still lodged in them, and lifted the bundle up to him. "And you won't be out there alone."

He took the pants and just as quickly dumped them on the floor. He reached for her arm instead and tugged her to her feet, closer to him.

With his arms around her waist, he leaned down and kissed her. Sweet and warm but not demanding.

He smiled when he lifted his head. "Did I ever tell you how beautiful you are?"

All the time. Joel wasn't one to hide his feelings. He'd told her repeatedly that he loved her and how much he wanted her. His expression would get all heated when he looked at her, and his breath would catch when he stripped her. The man knew how to convince a woman with words and actions how beautiful he found her.

He just didn't know how to stick around.

Rather than fight and ruin a perfectly good moment, she leaned into him. Her arms went to his neck and she brought him down for another kiss. "Yes, but feel free to say it again."

This kiss rumbled through her. When she thought he'd pull back, he deepened it, crossing his mouth over hers until a wave of dizziness hit her.

She ended it before poor Cam started banging on the door. "I like the way you use your mouth to make an argument. Very interesting, but I'm still coming with you."

"I figured as much." Joel smacked her butt and winked. "Get dressed."

When they stepped out on the porch five minutes later, Cam was already standing there with his fist raised as if about to knock. His gaze passed from Joel to Hope.

Cam swallowed a smile. "I can take another shift."

"Okay." Joel turned back into the cabin.

Hope ignored the flush of heat hitting her cheeks and grabbed him. "Joel, no."

"Fine." He stepped outside with a hand on her lower back and pulled the door shut behind them. "Anything happening out here?"

"Shuffling over there." Cam pointed at a shadowed spot to the far left of the cabins. "When I went to check it out I met a raccoon family."

Joel blew out a long ragged breath. "They know anything about the shooter?"

"If so, they're not talking." Cam yawned.

Joel shook his head as he grabbed Cam's flashlight. "Go to bed, you lightweight."

Hope took two steps off the porch and glanced around, looking for anything that might have changed from the nights before the retreat went haywire. Same logs and campfire area.

The front porch lights of each cabin remained off as Joel ordered. Turning them on would cast the world just a few feet out in total darkness, and that was too risky. So, they went with limited lighting and depended on their vision to adjust.

The night was still and the rain had slowed to a drizzle, so she lowered her hood. She could hear the dripping of water off the leaves. The soft ping of raindrops hitting the ground usually comforted her. Tonight it had an odd shiver shaking down her spine.

Something wasn't right. She'd spent so much of her life outside and could pick up on the strangeness of a moment. Her father joked she was one with nature, whatever that meant. Really, she had mentally catalogued the sights and sounds…and smells.

She turned around and the men stood right behind her. In her haze she hadn't heard them move.

Joel frowned. "What's going on?"

The scent. That was it. "Do you smell that?"

"I smell rain," Cam said.

Joel leaned past her in the direction of the cabin Cam was temporarily using and where Perry recuperated. "No, she's right."

Memories of her father's powerboat from when she was a little girl. The sharp scent she smelled every time she filled the tank of her car. "It's gasoline. Fire."

Joel was already running, with Cam right behind. They were shouting orders but she couldn't pick up the words as they got lost in the forest in front of them. They ran toward Perry's cabin.

Joel hit the door first. He reached for the knob and drew his hand back fast. Bending down, he rammed into the wood with his shoulder and it slammed open, bouncing against the inside wall.

He disappeared. Never hesitated. Never called for help. He just slipped in, stuck on hero mode like always.

Through the doorway she could see the orange flames licking up the inside back wall, and her heart shredded. Heat punched her in the face as smoke curled out of the opening and into the dark sky.

She tried to get her legs to move, but a sharp scream cut through her consciousness. It took another second to realize it came from her. Then Cam was in front of her with his hands on her shoulders.

He gave her a small shake. "We need water."

She grabbed fists full of his shirt and pulled. "Joel." His name ripped out of her.

"I'll get him, but I need water."

The comment refused to register in her brain.

Every cell screamed at her to rush in that door and hunt Joel down. "What?"

Cam put a hand on her cheek. "Hope, listen to me. We need to put this out before it spreads. It could take out all the cabins and us with it."

The cloud of confusion hovering around her cleared. Sparks caught on the breeze and drifted up into the sky in bright flashes of light. "There's a hose in the kitchen cabin. It's hooked to a well, but—"

"Go bang on Charlie's door. Wake him and everyone else up. We need all bodies on this."

A load roar had her looking past Cam into the cabin. She could make out a figure moving around. Her fingers tightened on Cam's shirt. "Get Joel out of there."

"I promise." He turned her toward Charlie's cabin. "Go."

Time blurred as she raced to the far cabin. Every step took forever, as if her legs weighed a thousand pounds each, and she yelled as she ran. By the time she hit the steps, the door opened and Charlie stood there in a white tank and shorts.

She ran right to him. "Fire!"

His eyes widened. "What?"

"We need everyone."

She didn't stay around to explain. She took off again. Her feet slid in the mud and she skidded across a patch of slick grass. Her balance faltered and her arms waved.

Out of the corner of her eye she saw a shadow looming near the doorway of the burning cabin. With her concentration gone, she slipped and fell, catching her weight on one arm before hitting the ground on her butt.

"Hope, are you okay?" Lance was right behind her, dragging her back to her feet with his hand under her arm.

His strength stunned her. The mild-mannered guy nearly picked her up with one hand. But her attention was on the scene in front of her. Joel staggered onto the porch with Perry hanging across his shoulders. Relief had her knees buckling. She would have fallen back to the ground if Lance wasn't holding her.

Joel got to the steps and flames shot up around him. The fire crackled and there was a loud bang from inside the cabin.

Hope needed to get to them. She took a step and ran into Jeff. He stood there, holding a blanket and staring blankly into the flaring orange.

Snatching it out of his hands, she rushed forward. She met Joel halfway down the stairs. The fire followed them. In a blind panic, she threw the blanket over Perry's body and patted out the flickers on his back and sleeve.

At the bottom and a good fifteen feet away

from the porch, Joel dropped to his knees. He rolled Perry off him and onto the ground. Joel followed a second later as he hacked and his body shook.

She slid down, ignoring the way the ground soaked her jeans and the residual pain from her knee injury. "Are you okay?"

A second coughing fit stopped whatever Joel was about to say. Slapping his hands against the ground, he turned around and got up on his hands and knees.

The noise plus the crackling of the fire drowned out his words. She looked up at him. "What?"

He put his hands over his mouth like a funnel. "Where are Charlie and Cam?"

Then she remembered the hose and the danger. Perry hadn't moved and Joel's skin was warm to the touch. Soot stained his forehead and she saw a hole in the back of his shirt where she guessed a spark had hit him.

"We need to get this fire out." She got up, thinking to grab Lance, until she felt a hand on her leg.

Looking down, she watched Joel use her for balance as he struggled to his feet. His chest caved from coughing, but his grip was strong. "We need a hose," he said over the shuddering cough.

"Cam is getting it." She pushed Joel farther from the fire and toward Jeff and cleaner air. "Lance and I will go."

Joel was already shaking his head. He pointed at the far side of the cabin. "We all go."

"What about Perry?" Lance asked as he stared at the still body.

"He's dead."

The sharp words stabbed into her. They'd lost Perry. It would have been Joel, too, if he'd stayed in the cabin another minute or two. Even now she heard wood break as the roof shifted.

She only shook herself out of the nightmare when Joel started moving. She reached for him just as she saw Cam and Charlie come around the corner with a hose and buckets.

Joel straightened as his coughing abated. "Everyone move."

"It won't reach," Cam called out the problem as he yanked on the thick hose dragging behind him. "We have to get this fire out now."

Charlie motioned to Lance and Jeff. "You two come with me and get the barrels."

She had no idea what that meant. Desperate to do something, she stood by Cam and Joel on the side of the fiery cabin and took over the job of spraying water. The hose was heavier than she'd expected and slipped through her hands twice, sending water shooting up and soaking her.

With a tighter grip, she tried again. This hose was nothing like one she'd seen in gardens. It was thicker and heavier. Heaving it under her arm, she aimed the stream at the flames peeking through the cabin wall.

As the flames grew, crashing thundered around them. The fire raged and more beams fell. More than once Joel and Cam stomped out small fires that jumped the cabin and took hold on the forest floor.

"Figures it's not raining now," Cam said.

Joel headed for the porch again. "We can't reach around to the front door and I need to get water in there. If I can get higher…"

When he eyed up the roof her gut twisted until she thought it would explode inside her. "No."

Cam sided with her and grabbed Joel just as he started to move. "No way. It's caving in. You'll go right down into the fire. Honestly, it will tick me off to have to go in after you."

"We don't have a choice."

"Shove something into the side. Make a hole." She screamed to be heard over the mix of fire and banging and water.

Both men stared at her.

She tried again. "Crash it in if you have to, just make an opening wide enough for me to get the water in."

This time they moved. After a quick look around, Joel motioned to the impossible-to-move logs they used as a seat around the fire pit. They each took an end and pulled.

She saw the strain on their faces and shaking in their arms. Somehow they carried it over to the cabin's side. Heat pulsed off the building in waves. Sweat rolled down her back, and her face felt on fire, like the worst, most intense sunburn ever.

On a count of three, with the muscles on their arms bulging from the staggering weight, they heaved the heavy piece of tree trunk at the wall. She waited until that exact minute and hit the buckling wood with a blast of water.

At first nothing happened. She held her breath and kept shooting the water. Then the crashing started. With a series of booms and thuds, a beam buckled. The roof side closest to them caved in and took a chunk of the wall tumbling down with it.

One minute she saw peeks of fire through the wall. The next it flared right in front of her. Scorching heat licked at her and then her back hit the ground.

The breath knocked out of her and the world went dark for a second. When she opened her eyes again, Joel's body pushed her into the mud as fire flashed over their heads.

Men yelled all around her. Over Joel's shoulder she saw Cam grab the abandoned hose and Charlie and Lance heave what looked like some sort of white powder at the fire. The joint hit had the flames lowering by a few feet.

She knew they weren't safe and the whole thing could explode. She searched her memory for anything incendiary inside the cabin and couldn't think of a thing.

Without another word, Joel helped her off the ground. In a line, working together, they all kept at the flames and doused any fires caused by sparks before they could burst into a new disaster.

No one mentioned how it could have started or pointed fingers. They were too busy trying not to be consumed by it.

TONY COULD FEEL the clock ticking as if it had been wound and placed in his brain. Connor had thrown his weight around and gotten Rafe all riled and demanding action. Now search parties had been set up. On Connor's orders, they were planning a hike to the campsite, rain or shine. Connor threatened to take a helicopter in even if it was raining.

Control had shifted and Tony no longer held the reins. After all the plotting, all those tedious hours of setting this up just right, one stupid woman had brought it all down. She didn't play the role he'd assigned her. Add in Connor and his group and it all fell apart.

Tony had planned this from the beginning. Step in, turn Baxter around and become its savior. When the sales numbers had come back soft, he'd waited. Then he'd seen preliminaries for a second quarter worse than the first and panicked.

He knew the work was there for Baxter. Piles of money just waited to flow his way, but he had to get the division in line with expectations. He had to dig more, push his staff harder. He needed time and bought it.

Then people got nosy and he had to regroup. The retreat had been the perfect way to settle things down. An accident and the game could reset.

Instead, Tony shoved pages into the shredder at four in the morning. His wife had called twice. She spent most of their weeknight dinners complaining about his long work hours.

Never mind that he worked around the clock for her. For the things he could give her and buy for her. That he had won her with his checkbook and the big house.

His trophy wife was slowly turning into a regular annoying one. He wanted pretty and obedient and understanding. A woman to wear on his arm and show off at the club. A blonde he'd enjoy in bed. One who would cause envious glares from his business associates. He'd had that for less than a year, and now he had the whining.

The shredder buzzed and the paper pulp dropped in the can underneath. He had a batch here and more at home. With his problem gone and the evidence erased, he could put the system back together again. The board might back off in deference to whatever was happening at the campground.

Tony could get his needed time, but it all depended on Connor not sticking his nose where it didn't belong. Making pages disappear and fudging numbers was one thing. Taking out a guy with a background in special ops was another.

No, Tony had to pull the plug. Shift the blame to another member of the executive staff. Plant the seed and focus the guilt elsewhere.

The idea came to Tony. If Mark was missing, maybe there was a reason he'd walked away, disappeared. Guilt. He'd played with the books to improve the look of his performance. He caused it all, did it all.

The more the idea spun in Tony's brain, the more he liked it. Turn Mark into the guilty party and then sit back and act surprised.

Tony pressed the button and stared at the stack of documents left in the file. He needed to spend his time recreating paperwork and making the trail. It would lead right back to his trusted vice president.

That meant Tony had to hold on to the money he'd syphoned off. Keep it hidden for now. Take everything underground until Connor and his team crawled back out of Baxter's business. The sooner that happened, the better.

Chapter Eleven

Hope had no idea how long they worked. Spraying the water, smothering the shorter bursts with blankets. They ran through all fire retardant Charlie had, but not before the flames had receded to a manageable level. It could have been an hour or minutes, but finally Cam waved them all back and went in with the hose to extinguish the last of the fire.

Exhausted, she dropped to the ground and sat. Some of the men joined her, and Joel sat by her side with his legs out in front of him and his shoulders slumped.

No one spoke as they studied the burnt-out char that once had been a cabin. Smoke still hung in the air and they all took turns coughing. The red sky had given way to a soft gray. Hope knew that meant sunrise wasn't that far away.

Jeff was the first to say anything. He sat with his legs bent and feet on the ground as he dragged a stray stick through the mud. "So, what, Perry woke up long enough to set a fire?"

Lance shrugged. "Could be guilt."

It never dawned on her that Perry could have done this. Last she knew he was unconscious. She was about to point that out when Joel squeezed his hand over her knee.

"He was missing. Mark's still missing. Maybe the two of them had a fight and something happened." Lance rubbed his hand over his wound. "Perry's the type who couldn't live with it if something happened, even by accident."

"An autopsy will tell us," Cam said as he returned with Charlie from turning off and replacing the hose.

Nearly hitting Lance, Jeff threw the stick. "How are we going to get one of those out here?"

"He means later." Joel stood and put a hand down to help her up. "We're putting together something to carry Perry's body. Once we get a bit more light, we can leave for the open field."

The plan sounded like heaven to her, so she started mentally preparing a list of things they needed. Two items of guilt piled on her, pushing her down into the cloying mud. The baggage, the loss of Perry, it all stacked up on top of the guilt from Mt. Ranier.

Mark was her responsibility and he was still lost. He could be the cause of all this, but he could also be a victim. Celebrating walking out of there while Mark stayed behind filled her with a blinding uncertainty.

"Take only what we need. Someone can come back for the rest later." Like, after they figured out who did what and when and tracked down Mark. In the scheme of priorities, "things" didn't matter.

They had all started moving when Jeff broke in again. "What about the sniper?"

"We'll go a different way." Joel grabbed Hope's knife off the ground and handed it to her.

She had no idea where or when she had dropped it. Likely in the middle of all the bucket carrying and blanket smothering, but who knew?

"Won't the sniper, or Mark, or whoever this is, just follow us?" Jeff's voice rose an octave as he talked.

"No." Hope knew about the riggings and had a good idea where Joel's head was on this.

Perry didn't start that fire because he was unconscious, which meant it was likely one of the people standing here did. She could rule out three and didn't want to take her chances with the rest.

"No offense, but I'm not just going to believe your gut. Or his." Jeff pointed at Joel.

For the second time since they'd met, the men were in a standoff. Joel was taller, younger and fitter. This battle would be no contest, but Jeff didn't seem to realize that fact.

She did. "Jeff, this isn't a good idea."

But he talked right over her. "That's what this is, right? You think you can somehow dodge a bullet."

Joel waited, letting Jeff's agitated comment ring in the air before responding. "Are you done? If so, let's move."

Lance raised a hand. "I'm in."

"I have some stuff I need to grab, and some food and supplies, just in case, but so am I." Charlie left right after he made his informal vote.

"Want to stay out here and take your chances, Jeff?" Joel nodded at the blanket that now covered Perry's body. "Because he's coming along."

Jeff shook his head. "No, we should—"

"Enough arguing. Rain or shine, we're moving. There's a helicopter and a radio and our team."

"Team?"

Joel talked right over Jeff's shout. "The storms stopped. We're down to light rain, and I say we can at least get out of this area and to somewhere safer and warm."

Cam nodded. "As the pilot, I agree."

"This plan is insane," Jeff said.

She had taken just about enough. She stepped in between Joel and Jeff and stared the businessman down. "We've been shot at, there's been a fire, Perry is dead and Mark is still missing. Staying here is insane."

"We'll deal with all of this once we're at the helicopter," Joel said.

"I have two tents." She was sure she had other supplies, but those came to her first.

Joel's expression stayed blank as he glanced at her. "For what?"

"In case we can't take off and need to set up in the open field."

"I can't believe this." Jeff turned around in a huff. He faced the shadowed forest, then started pacing.

"Again, you're welcome to stay here." Joel caught Jeff's arm and stopped the march. "But we're leaving."

"Fine," Jeff said through clenched teeth.

Hope didn't realize she was holding her breath until Jeff finally said the word. Relief and fear and a few emotions she couldn't name swept over her. She vowed to sleep for a week after this was over…if it ever ended.

But first they had to survive it. "Let's get ready to move out."

THE SUN HADN'T risen, but Joel was already out of patience. The lighter sky made it possible to dodge upturned branches and other potential hazards on the forest floor. He took the lead with his weapon ready. Cam brought up the rear. The responsibility fell to Jeff and Charlie to carry the sleeping bag with Perry inside.

Hope guided their new path. Using her GPS, she veered off the rough trail campers used to lead them to the open space where the helicopter sat. They knew from experience there were weapons rigged and ready to shoot that way. Worries about those riggings being everywhere had Joel constantly looking into the trees and tripping over whatever he missed on the ground.

"Why don't we go the way we know?" Charlie asked through labored pants.

"Because the shooter might also know that way." Joel didn't even want to share that much. He kept his tone clipped and angry, hoping to end the discussion.

"But we could end up anywhere."

"We're fine." Hope kept her gaze on the GPS as she shifted them through overgrown branches and around felled trees.

"Doesn't feel like it," Jeff mumbled as he shuffled his feet and grumbled about the weight of the sleeping bag.

"We could probably do without the whining." Joel decided he could go a lifetime without that.

"You're not the one carrying a dead body for miles."

"A mile." Hope made a tsk-tsking sound. "Don't exaggerate."

Joel felt safe smiling because no one could see him but Hope and she was looking off to her left, deep into the forest. "Would you rather no one check for snipers?"

Next time anyone asked him to head out and help babysit a bunch of weekend warriors, he'd find something else to do. Unless it meant being with Hope. He'd always choose the option that led to her.

It would shred him into pieces to leave her again. Sleeping with her guaranteed that, but he had been a dead man before that anyway. He saw her and he lost his mind. He spent time with her and he started thinking impossible things. For about the billionth time since he'd met her, he wished he was a different man from a different background.

"I can help." Lance slid his pack off his good shoulder and held it out to Hope. "Can you take this?"

"Sure." She grabbed it with her free hand. Never mind the fact that she already had one strapped to her back.

Joel tried to do the calculation. He stopped when the number got too high. At this rate she could be dragging more than she weighed.

He reached over and took Lance's pack from her. "I'll take it."

"I'm a big girl, Joel. I can carry a second bag."

Not that he let that stop him. If one of them was

going to carry two bags, it would be him, not her. "Unlike Jeff, I totally believe in your skills."

"Uh-huh." She was squinting and didn't seem to be listening. Not her style at all.

He crowded in closer and leaned down to whisper in her ear. "You okay?"

"Not really."

He tried to keep one eye on her and the other on the area ahead. A second of lost concentration could cost them all. Still, he needed her on her game. "Do you need to stop for a—"

"We left Mark behind."

There it was. The blame he knew she was shouldering. Her eyes were big and sad when they stared up at him. The pain he saw there nearly broke him. "Don't take that on."

Confusion mixed with the rest. "What?"

"The guilt."

She visibly swallowed as she looked away. The ground thumped beneath them as they continued to walk. "He's my job. I guaranteed his safety and promised to bring him home."

"And I'm an expert at this sort of thing. Trust me, if there's blame to be had here, other than to Mark for wandering off in the first place, it goes on my shoulders."

"Why?"

"I was sent to make sure something like this didn't happen, and it did. On my watch."

Her steps faltered as her foot hit a loose root. "You always do that."

"What?"

"Take on everyone's pain."

He knew it wasn't true. If anything he shied away from emotional connections. He kept a cool head and a distance. The combination made him good at his job. And lousy at his relationship with her.

"I can handle it." He'd been trained to shoulder the responsibility.

In his father's world, the men had to step up and do what had to be done. Most of what the man said was a convoluted mess of craziness, but Joel internalized the need to step up and he wouldn't apologize for that.

"So can I," she said.

Joel pitched his voice even lower. "I know, but I don't want you to."

It was killing him not to touch her then. He could hear the buzz of conversation behind him, most of it complaining from Jeff. They were not alone.

"We need to head to the right. There's a better path over there," Charlie called out from near the back of the pack.

Hope shook her head. "That swings us too far over."

"It's the best way," Charlie insisted.

She kept her focus on the GPS screen. "We're fine. We're not far now."

"I'd rather trust Charlie on this since he owns the campground. *He* knows these woods," Jeff said.

"This time Jeff's right," Charlie agreed.

Joel wasn't in the mood to encourage their ramblings. He heard Cam settling everyone down, which was good because Hope kept frowning.

"Look to your left." She looked straight as she said the words. "Don't draw attention, but look. What's that about thirty feet out by the small hill?"

"A mound of dirt and leaves." Her eyesight was perfect. Joel questioned his because he had to narrow his gaze, homing in on the spot she indicated. "All stacked under a lean-to."

He also saw something red. A piece of material, maybe. The storm had blown apart someone's hiding place, and there was no question something was buried under there.

"Maybe the wind pushed it all up there during the storm."

If she needed to believe that to get through the next few hours, he'd let it happen. "Is that what you think?"

She nibbled on her bottom lip. "What are you thinking?"

That she might have found Mark and, if so,

the man was not their attacker. Only bad news no matter how you looked at it. "You don't want to know."

"We should look."

"I can't spread any more panic." Joel caught her hand when he thought she'd peel off and check out the site on her own. "Note the coordinates on your GPS and move us to the east so the others don't see."

"Do you really think—"

"Get us to the clearing as fast as you can, but take us out around this site."

Before she could say anything else, Joel dropped back, hanging along the right side of the group and hoping to bring their attention with him and away from the find on the left. He answered one of Lance's questions, though Joel would never be able to remember what he'd said if someone asked him later.

He drew next to Cam, impressed at the clip Hope had them moving in now on the rough terrain. After working with him, Joel didn't have to clue Cam in to the existence of a problem.

Cam kept his gaze straight and dropped his voice low. "What's wrong?"

"Behind you to the left, thirty or so feet."

"The pile." Cam nodded. "Want me to check it out?"

"Do you need to?" They had had the same training, had seen many of the same things.

Cam took a second to study it. "Probably not." Joel was about to rejoin Hope when the concern in Cam's voice stopped him. "Be careful up there. I don't like you in front of this group."

That made two of them. "Watch my back."

"Done."

About ten minutes later they broke through the thick cover of trees and hit the edge of the woods on the opposite side from where he'd gone into the forest when they first arrived. The open expanse of the clearing stretched in front of them. The helicopter sat shining despite the overcast morning skies.

Joel brought the group to a halt under the cover of the final line of trees and scanned the area.

The space provided the perfect place for an ambush. Anyone could be hiding anywhere. A weapon could be pointed at them right now.

Lance dropped his side of the makeshift gurney and double-timed his steps as if he was running to freedom. Cam caught him in mid-stride. "Hold up."

"What?" Lance's gaze bounced from Cam to Hope.

She gave him a shaky smile. "It's going to be okay. Just be patient."

Joel didn't feel the need to sugarcoat it. "We don't know who else is out here, so do not move."

Charlie's head came up. "Wait a second."

With Cam's help, Charlie and Jeff lowered the sleeping bag the rest of the way to the ground.

Lance kept shifting his weight back and forth as if he was ready to bolt. "So we're going to just stand here?"

"What's the plan?" Charlie asked at the same time.

Joel had met more grateful rescuees before. Then again, he'd had some with even bigger attitudes. The protection business wasn't always an easy gig. "As Hope said, patience."

Cam stepped up. "I'll go."

No way was Joel letting that happen. If anyone ran out there, it would be him. He'd dragged Cam along on this gig, promising a quick stop, and ended up dropping him into the middle of a disaster. "We're not sacrificing you."

Charlie threw up his hands. "Someone has to get out there and call for help."

"You're clear of the trees. Can't you use your satphone?" Hope asked.

"It's on the helicopter." Not the best topic as far as Joel was concerned.

When they first left the helicopter, he figured he'd be right back. When they came a second time, he was more interested in the gear and extra guns. He'd screwed up, and Cam gave him crap for it.

Not that the sat phone would have been of any use until right now anyway. Like hers, his needed a clear shot at the sky, and between the trees and the weather, he hadn't had that for two days.

"I'm going." Cam slipped off his pack. "Cover me."

He took two steps and a shot rang out. His body went down. Hitting the ground on his stomach, he didn't move.

Hope gasped and the men started shouting. Joel refused to lose it. A single shot and a spiderweb of broken glass on the helicopter windshield. That put the shot high and likely from the direction of the old location.

Still, his voice shook as he called out, "Cam?"

"What?" He didn't move as he answered.

Joel let the relief wash through him. As expected, Cam had fallen more out of training and experience than anything else. "It's the rigging."

"You sure?" Cam put his palms against the ground and pushed up enough to glance back at Joel. "I'd really hate for you to be wrong here."

Hope shook her head. "But no one is standing over there to trip it."

"There could be another one on this side." Joel looked behind him, trying to find it.

"What are you two talking about?" Lance asked.

The other men wore similar confused expressions. Joel understood the frustration and need to know, but this wasn't the time. And if his suspicions were correct, one of them might already know.

"I'm getting up." Cam shifted as he spoke.

Joel wasn't about to leave him out there unprotected. He pushed into the open, breaking the tree line and glancing back into the forest. He scanned the area for movement as well as riggings, just in case.

Nothing spiked his radar. "Go."

He heard the pounding of feet and saw Cam race past him at full speed. Jeff jumped back and Hope tried to catch him. Cam ceased his momentum with a rather large tree. His hands hit the bark and his feet stopped.

Hope went right to him, running her hands over his back and arms. "Are you okay?"

Cam glanced at Joel. "Fine."

"What is that?" Jeff cowered as a thwapping sound split through the otherwise quiet morning.

The helicopter cleared the trees and headed for the clearing. There was enough room to land, but it would take some skill. Good thing the Corcoran Team had plenty of that.

"The cavalry." Forget panic. Other than the rain finally stopping, this was the first good news they'd had in days.

"Your team?"

The hope in her eyes nearly did Joel in. "Yeah."

The helicopter kicked up wind, and the noise drowned out all other sounds. The trees around the open space swayed and the grass flattened. It felt like forever before it touched down and the propellers slowed.

Joel took one step into the clearing and held up a hand. After a few more minutes, the helicopter wound down.

Connor leaned out and yelled. "What's wrong?"

Joel appreciated the boss's caution. "We just took fire. Could be a rigged weapon."

Connor nodded and then moved back inside for a second. When he came out it was with guns up and two men helping. Joel recognized one—Corcoran's second in command, Davis Weeks, a man Joel would serve beside and trust with Hope's safety any day.

When they ran across the area without another shot being fired, Joel figured it was safe. He met Connor with a handshake about ten feet from the edge of the clearing. "About time you got here."

"I had to break about a dozen laws and ignore the screaming from the guy at a nearby airport and a police chief to get here." Connor hitched his thumb in the other guy's direction. "Davis came along to fly the plane and we picked up a ranger."

Joel knew they could all fly but didn't question

the extra man. Only issue was getting them all out, but that was Connor's problem. "Thanks for that. Both of you."

Connor slid his gun back into the holster. "I almost hate to ask, but who's in the bag?"

"Better yet, who's the woman?" Davis asked.

"Perry, one of the Baxter executives." Joel motioned for the rest of the group to join them. "And this is Hope Algier."

Davis smiled at Joel. "Her father is not happy with you."

"He's the one who sent me out here."

"We'll talk about how you spend your vacations later." Connor walked past Joel to welcome the group.

Davis leaned in. "And we'll definitely talk about the woman."

Chapter Twelve

Hope barely made it to her town house that night before falling over. She'd gotten to know Connor and Davis as they kept up a steady stream of mindless chatter on the helicopter ride out of the forest. They talked about a debriefing but gave her a day's reprieve on having to sit through it. Apparently she had paperwork to fill out and questions to answer.

They promised they'd take care of the inevitable search for Mark and investigation into Perry's death. She was grateful, but there was so much information to take in. It all welled up until it threatened to choke her.

At one point she had to concentrate on her breathing to keep from putting her head between her knees to calm down. And she wasn't the scare-easily type.

She always held it together. Or she had done so until her life fell apart in the double whammy of losing Joel and losing her climbing guide career.

Back at the airport hangar, when Joel had announced the coordinates she'd marked off in the forest and suggested it could be a grave site—presumably Mark's—her stomach had dipped. She'd known what he thought when they were out there. Hearing the stark truth as he delivered the news to his colleagues sliced through her.

When the cavernous room had started to spin away from her, Joel had held her hand and told her everything would be fine. But it was Davis with his photos of his pregnant wife that took her mind off all the death.

The big man seemed to be totally in love. He grinned as he pointed and his voice picked up with excitement. Hope found his happiness contagious.

The talk also filled her with a strange sadness. A longing for what she feared she'd never have. She couldn't exactly move on and start a new life when she was still stuck in the old one. The main part of which was rummaging around in her kitchen right now.

"I take it you're staying here tonight?" she asked as she sat down across from him.

Joel froze with his hand on the open refrigerator door. "I don't want to drive back to Annapolis."

Never mind that the rest of his team found somewhere to sleep in the DC area. He hadn't even asked. Just drove her to the town house and settled in.

Truth was he was here and she wasn't about to kick him out. Didn't even want to try. "Fair enough."

He shut the door and came around the kitchen island to where she sat on a high barstool. Her bare feet dangled off the footrest. She'd showered and changed into clean clothes, consisting of a thin T-shirt, which had his gaze skipping to her breasts every few seconds, and plaid boxer shorts.

She'd chosen the outfit on purpose. To entice him. Some men loved to see women in tight skirts or sexy lingerie. Joel preferred the fresh, down-home look. Put on something he could tunnel his hands under, maybe no underwear and just a hint of the bare skin beneath, and he lost his cool. Happened every time.

She wasn't the only one who showered. So had he, but he'd used her downstairs bathroom instead of the one in her bedroom upstairs.

The restraint surprised her. She had half expected him to pull back the curtain and step in with her. Not that she would have objected, though the dressed version was pretty nice and smelled pretty good, too.

Damp hair, faded jeans and a white tee that slipped over him like a second skin. Looked like he also knew how to entice.

Right now he did it by stepping into the space between her legs. He didn't touch her. Didn't have to. The place was small enough for her to feel his presence in every room, even though he hadn't lived there in months.

The end unit had two bedrooms and a small office. The entire place could fit into the guesthouse at her father's place, but the size was perfect for her. She liked cozy and her oversize sectional sofa that dwarfed the rest of the family room. The shelves loaded with books and the collection of mismatched coffee mugs she collected from her travels.

Her dad liked shiny knickknacks and marble floors. He had money and enjoyed spending it. She didn't begrudge him the wealth or the power. It didn't define him. Certainly didn't say anything about him as a dad, and he was a good one. Overprotective with a tendency to butt in, but his heart was in the right place. He wanted her happy and insisted Joel was the man for her.

She didn't disagree.

Joel stood in front of her now and slid his palms up her shorts, skimming his fingers underneath to touch bare skin. "Do you want me to leave?"

There was no reason to play games. They loved each other and hurt each other. It was a vicious cycle, but one she couldn't break. "No."

"Is it too forward to say I have condoms in my duffel bag?" He kissed her cheek, then his mouth traveled to her ear.

She tilted her head to give him greater access. The man could kiss, and when he kissed her there her body trembled with excitement.

Her hands came up and she held on to his upper arms for balance. "More wishful thinking?"

"Just good planning." He said the comment and it vibrated against her skin.

Her eyes, already half closed, popped open again. She pulled back, almost breaking contact, and stared at him. "I don't get it."

"Davis put them in there when he packed the bag."

The married man with a pregnant wife was carrying condoms? "I don't know what to say to that."

"They were totally for my benefit. He got the briefing on you."

The conversation was sucking some of the life out of the seduction scene. "Meaning?"

Instead of answering, Joel dipped his head and kissed her, and the seduction was back on. The rush of longing hit her so hard she would have fallen off the stool if his hands weren't on her hips.

Even with the adrenaline and danger gone, she still craved him. The feelings kicked into high gear when she'd convinced herself they'd fade.

When he lifted his head, she traced a finger over his bottom lip. "Nice."

"He knows...they all do now, my whole team..." Joel kissed her nose. "...what you mean to me."

Her heart flipped. Actually felt as if it had torn loose and performed a perfect somersault. "Which is?"

"Everything."

And that was it. The doubt fled and the need for self-preservation wavered. He had given her the words that broke open the gates and made her want to try again.

She knew in her soul he believed them, felt them. She hoped he'd follow through this time, but reality nipped at her on that one.

But none of the "what ifs" and "what about tomorrows" mattered right then. His fingers brushed the insides of her legs to her upper thighs, and his hot mouth pressed against hers. She wanted him—over her, with her, inside her.

"Come upstairs with me." She whispered the plea against his mouth.

The kiss deepened and the room spun. One minute she was on the barstool and the next he stood with her body wrapped around his.

She linked her ankles and let her legs ride low on his hips. His erection pressed against her, and his deep breathing filled her head. When he walked, taking them across the room, the movement barely registered.

Somehow he got them to the couch. He stood hovering over it, without ever breaking the contact of their mouths or stilling his hands as they traveled all over her back.

When he sat down, her knees pressed into the couch cushions on either side of his hips. Her fingers went into his hair as his hands slipped under her shirt and up her back.

"I'm happy you were at camp." Her lips pressed against his throat.

His head tipped back. "I hated the idea of you out there without me."

"It's my job."

He cupped her cheeks with his palms and looked deep into her eyes. "I want you safe."

Her hand trailed down his flat stomach to his lap. She could feel the heat pounding off him and into her. His erection pressed against the notch between her legs and he kept shifting, driving in closer.

When he moved again, she unbuttoned his jeans. He hadn't bothered with a belt and as she lowered the zipper, she knew he hadn't put on underwear either. How very practical of him.

Her hand slid over him, and her mouth brushed over his. "Take me to bed."

Hands clenched against her outer thighs. "I thought you'd never ask."

It was after nine as Tony walked to the head of the conference room table and sat down. His men had experienced days of difficulty and hardship. Their numbers had been shaved from four to two. They wore the horror of the experience on their faces. Both Jeff and Lance were pale and drawn. Neither gave Tony eye contact.

He suspected they wanted to go home and forget everything that had happened. He couldn't exactly blame them. He wanted to erase the past few days from his memory, too.

On his orders, both had been checked out at the hospital at length. Despite the ordeal, they were healthy physically. But he wanted to assess the emotional part. He also needed to know what they knew.

Everyone wanted to interview them, from the police to the park rangers to Connor to the press. Tony wanted to secure them and lock them away, but he knew that wasn't practical. As it was, he had managed to buy a little time, citing their raw state. But the clock was ticking.

He knew he'd lose the battle when it came to Connor. The man appeared to take the lead on the entire investigation, and no one in the police department or any federal agency objected or tried to push the man aside. He walked in and they stepped back.

As suspected, Connor and his team were trouble. Hope and this guy Joel were the worst. Their names kept coming up, so Tony placed the blame for his pounding headache and the twisting in his gut solely on them.

But he had to deal with that later. Right now he had more bad news to deliver. The kind of news that broke men, or at least started them on a vigilante crusade. Tony didn't want any part of either of those things. He needed these two healthy and indebted to him. Supporting him.

"After they got you out, search and rescue found a body in the woods." The news, though expected, still had stunned Tony when Connor called to tell him.

With everything that had gone wrong, this part had gone as planned.

Jeff slumped forward, balancing his elbows on the table. "What?"

"Mark."

Lance shook his head. "Did Perry do it?"

"We think so." Or that was the story that worked best for this new scenario Tony had concocted.

Mark was supposed to have an accident. Walk off into the woods and fall off a mountainside or fall and hit his head. The fact that he was buried under a pile of leaves made that tough to sell.

"Perry wouldn't hurt Mark." Jeff looked to Lance. "Right?"

Last thing Tony needed was these two teaming up and exchanging stories. "You need to know the rest. After you left camp, I discovered some financial irregularities."

Jeff dipped even lower in his chair. "What does that mean?"

"It looks like Mark was inflating his numbers to make the new division look like it was performing better than it was." The evidence now supported the claims. Notes and files, all backdated and slipped into computer backups using earlier dates. It paid to have a staff of tech experts who passed on their expertise. Tony had learned a thing or two over the years.

"That explains the information I collected," Jeff said.

Tony forced his expression to stay neutral. "What are you talking about?"

"Inconsistent performance in one of our divisions, the newest. I thought it might be an aberration but wanted to get at the issue in case the dip in productivity and revenue was a signal of things to come."

"You didn't come to me with this?" Tony couldn't keep the menace out of his voice. He knew that when Lance glanced up and his eyes narrowed.

"I talked with Mark about marketing strategies we could use to stabilize the numbers." Jeff frowned. "I thought he had talked about that with you."

That answered that question. Tony worried Mark had shared the information he compiled with other members of the staff. Looked like Jeff was the source and went to Mark, who listened to the concerns but didn't play his own hand or express his suspicions about what was going on. Mark ran to Tony, never mentioning Jeff, and everything rolled downhill from there.

The poor decision-making by Mark to take credit for Jeff's findings and keep the matter quiet made it easier for Tony to lay the trail. He placed a few more tracks now. "The real problem is the reason behind the instability."

Lance stopped tapping his hand against the table long enough to stare. "What do you mean?"

"It looks as if Mark had created a pretty elaborate scheme. He set up false client accounts and funneled money into them. The initial moving of money showed up as a down quarter in performance when, really, he was pocketing portions of money we received. He tried to cover everything up with inflated numbers after the fact, making it look as if he'd saved the division, but it was too late." When Tony realized he was swiveling his chair back and forth, he stopped. He needed calm and reassurance right now. The nerves rattling inside him couldn't show.

Lance shook his head. "That can't be right."

"I'm afraid it is." Tony rushed to dispel any

thoughts of questioning him. "The only logical explanation is Perry found out and paid for his loyalty to this company with his life."

"I can't believe this," Jeff said.

"You're lucky it wasn't you. My guess is you were next." Tony thought back to the last document he had created. "I guess that explains why he sent me the memo asking for the corporate retreat. To get all of you out there and provide cover as he hid his hand in this."

"But then who killed Mark?" Lance flattened his hand against the table and leaned forward as he talked.

He still wore the sling from the injury he'd sustained in the woods. Something about a sniper or a rigged gun. Tony didn't know about any of that but planned to find out.

Tony shrugged. "My guess is Perry."

That was the new plan—implicate both men. Invent a scenario where they turned on each other. Mark lost in his lying and Perry trying to get at the truth. It played well, and Tony found it easier than continuing to hide the losses.

He could spin this into betrayal and vow to fix the corporate tendency that led to it. Overhaul the whole reporting process and means of calculating overhead.

In the end, the ruse could streamline the company and preserve the bottom line. And that would secure his position and the bonuses he needed.

But Lance didn't appear to be buying the story. The lowest man on the corporate leadership ladder kept shaking his head, skepticism apparent on his face. "This is going round in circles."

"The important thing is we're back on track." The man would need convincing, and Tony vowed to do just that. But not today. They all needed to stand down and get some breathing room on this. Tony also needed to handle Connor and the Corcoran Team, which looked like it could be a full-time job. "These men's families deserve to believe in them. We'll walk a careful line, clean this up and move on."

"The board is in agreement with that strategy?" Jeff asked.

"We'll work it out. Everything will be legal and transparent, but respectful to the dead." As soon as he had a report to present Tony would start that process.

The board, reeling from the loss of two executives, wasn't pressuring him for anything other than answers about their deaths. The financial issue wasn't on their radar. He'd put it there but in his own way. The way he needed it to look.

"In the meantime, you two should take a week. To the extent you need any assistance in terms of counseling or additional medical issues, Baxter will, of course, cover everything."

"Thanks," Jeff said, but Lance stayed quiet.

They'd all had enough for one night, and the next few days would be rough. There were funerals to plan and a story to spin out. "Now go home."

With a minimum of shuffling, both men got up. They exchanged thank you's and shook hands before he sent them out the door. Tony gritted his teeth through the entire spiel. He wasn't accustomed to explaining anything to anyone. He gave orders and people followed them. Now with Mark gone and the information buried with him, Tony could get back to the business of running Baxter.

Through the glass door, he saw Lance and Jeff head out for the night. Tony waved and smiled even as the cell in his jacket pocket buzzed for the fourth time in less than a half hour. He knew who was calling. Knew and ignored it because this was the one problem he hadn't counted on.

Tony glanced at the cell screen. He recognized the number because it had popped up all day. The texts, the voicemails. If his unwanted partner was trying to create a discoverable trail, he was doing a great job. The covert part of their relationship seemed to be confusing the man at the moment.

Tony would explain and set it straight, but not now. He needed a few minutes of quiet to think.

The man would come calling soon. And Tony would be ready.

Chapter Thirteen

The next morning Joel watched Connor do the two things he did every day—sit at the head of a conference room table and pour coffee. Only today, the table wasn't his table, and neither was the business. This office space and all the resources they needed were on loan from Algier Security, but that didn't seem to faze Connor or make him look any less in charge.

He poured a cup for Hope, then dropped the pot on the tray in front of him, leaving Davis and Joel to fend for themselves. After a night in Hope's bed, making love with her, holding her, Joel didn't need the kick.

But Connor was a caffeine addict. Could put away a pot in an hour and keep going back all day. Joel often wondered if he slept.

Since Connor's wife had moved out and he refused to talk about why or where she was, Joel doubted it. Connor still wore his wedding ring and referred to Jana all the time.

At first he insisted she was visiting a relative, but as the months dragged on it became obvious the marriage had imploded. He didn't even bother to try to explain anymore.

Joel chalked it up to one more example of how a relationship couldn't work long term with this job. Everyone agreed Jana and Connor were the perfect couple. Smart, focused, dedicated to each other and the work. And now she was gone.

"Your father is letting us use his office as our satellite office," Connor explained to Hope.

She smiled over the rim of her mug. "Sounds like Dad."

"He's on the way back home and not happy he got stuck because of weather and couldn't be here to meet you." Joel knew because he'd had two long, yelling phone calls from the man already this morning. The second ended with an order to marry Hope and be done with it.

With all his power and money, Rafe Algier had a very basic agenda. He wanted his only child safe and he wanted her with Joel. Both options worked for Joel except that he couldn't figure out how to make the second stick without endangering the first.

As if she had read his mind, she slid her hand under the table and rested her hand on his knee. "I'm fine."

The simple touch sent fire racing through him. That's all it took. "I'll make sure you stay that way."

"On that note…" Davis looked at his watch for the tenth time since they'd all gotten there a half hour ago and gotten the video feed hooked up to the Corcoran Team offices. "I'm thinking I should move out to headquarters. I'll coordinate from Annapolis. Use our resources and Joel's impressive computer programs to get through all the information we've collected."

"I'd ask you not to touch my stuff, but—"

Davis nodded. "I'm going to anyway."

"When is your wife due?" Hope asked.

"Lara." Davis smiled as he said her name, just as he always did. "And she's a little more than five months along."

"He doesn't like to be away from her." Joel knew he was stating the obvious, but he did it anyway.

"True, but I also want to be back in our office, helping Pax and Ben analyze the data." Davis winked at Hope. "Being with my wife is just a huge bonus."

"Who are the other men you mentioned?" Hope's hand slid off Joel's leg.

He put it back on his thigh again. "Members of the team. There are a few others who mostly work with Cam, but they're on enforced leave right now."

"Enforced?"

"I demanded they take some downtime because they travel all the time," Connor said. "Cam happened to be available and can fly, so he headed out to drop Joel off with you."

"Which didn't go so well for me," Cam pointed out as he slipped into the room and took the seat next to Davis.

"Okay then." She exhaled as she took another sip of coffee. "I think I'm caught up now."

"I'm sure we'll lose you a second or third time," Cam said. "Sorry I'm late."

"Why are you?" Joel asked.

"Checking the helicopter." When Connor started to talk, Cam waved him off. "It's fine and the front window is being fixed. We'll be able to use it as soon as you're ready."

Joel wanted to ask what for, but Cam looked at him and gave a small shake of his head. Whatever the mission was, it looked like it was off the books for Connor. That only intrigued Joel more.

Hope wrapped her hand around her mug. "At the risk of ruining any image you may have of me as a smart person, let me ask what could be an obvious question. Why do you need an office here at all? Why not just head home now that I'm away from the campground?"

Home. The word knocked around in Joel's brain. It meant leaving her. "The job isn't over."

True, it was an informal one, but Rafe made it clear Corcoran had been hired to figure out what went wrong on the retreat. He wanted answers and some assurance his daughter would not be put in jeopardy again.

Joel wanted the same thing, and Connor didn't even blink at the request. He might have lost his wife, but he was deadly loyal to the team. If one of them needed something, Connor stepped in.

The light in Hope's eyes dimmed a bit. "I still can't believe Mark is dead."

Joel squeezed her hand. "Thanks to you spotting him, we were able to recover his body quickly."

All of the men nodded. Davis looked more than a little impressed. Joel wondered what he'd say if he knew about all of her skills.

"Forensics teams are swarming all over the place," Connor said.

Cam half stood up and reached across the table for the coffeepot. "Why aren't we there?"

"Jurisdictional nonsense, but we get a look at everything. Raw data, samples whatever we need."

Davis chuckled. "You convinced the police to do that?"

Connor smiled. "I can be very persuasive."

Some of the building tension that came with talking about tough subjects seeped out of the room, but Hope continued to frown. "I still don't get the outpost here."

"Baxter is in town and I want to be where Tony Prather is right now." Connor's smile grew, as if he relished the idea of going to battle with this guy. "Let him know I haven't forgotten him or the promise I made to solve this mystery."

"Plus we have two murders and an explanation that's half-as—"

She chuckled over Davis's sudden stoppage. "Yes?"

He cleared his throat. "Let's go with unbelievable."

Cam nodded. "Nice save."

"The Perry versus Mark fight Tony is trying to sell doesn't hold together." Connor scanned the notes in front of him. "How could Perry start the fire in his condition and why would he?"

Joel filled in the blanks in case she didn't follow the jumping conversation. As a group they sometimes talked in shorthand and forgot to cut that out when others joined in. "We all know Perry was out of it. Cam checked on him about ten minutes before you smelled gasoline, and the guy was out cold."

"So, supposedly Perry sprang up and was oriented and stable enough to go find gas, which he hadn't used up until then, pour it all over the cabin, light the match, then lie back down and go to sleep." Cam snorted. "I don't think so."

Davis shrugged. "The police buy it."

Hope's mug hit the table with a sharp whack. "Come on, really?"

"Tony Prather tells a good story. The man is a natural salesman, after all," Connor said.

"He didn't do anything for me. And this is the same executive who didn't go along on the executive retreat even though he set it up?" She added an eye roll to the end.

"Wait, go back." Connor stilled. "Tony insists Mark is the one who wanted the retreat."

"That's not what Tony told me when we talked about what he wanted on this job." She took out her cell and started scrolling. When she landed on a specific email, she turned the phone and showed Connor. "I asked why he wasn't coming along and he gave me some excuse about not being able to take time away from running the company but said it was necessary for everyone else for morale and team building."

"The guy is slippery." Connor finished reading and then passed the cell phone to Davis. "Tony didn't want to send out a search team and didn't seem all that concerned about Mark or motivated to get out there for a rescue."

"A great guy all around." Davis slid the phone back to her.

She put it in front of Joel and returned her hand to his knee. "But why do all of this? The executive retreat is a lot of trouble."

"With a lot of moving parts." That's the point Joel didn't understand.

If you wanted to get rid of an executive or pit two against each other, there had to be easier ways. Out in the forest the control vanished. There was the human element, plus weather and animals and accidents. The list went on and on.

Connor rested his elbows on the table and reached over to refill his already empty coffee cup. "I think we're looking at the oldest reason in the world—money."

She groaned as she rubbed her eyes. "I was afraid you'd say that."

"With the help of a skeptical member of the board who didn't want Tony hired in the first place, Ben has been back at Corcoran headquarters digging through the Baxter records. He's had access to notes and files and reports so boring your head would spin," Davis explained.

"How'd he get stuck with the job?" she asked as a smile tugged at the corner of her mouth.

"Newest member." Joel had been in that unenviable position and celebrated when someone came in after him.

He was no longer the new guy, though he often felt that way. Still getting his footing and learning along the way. He knew the basic skills coming in and could match, or beat, any of them at shooting and tracking, but strategies and tactics were a different skill set. Connor and Davis excelled at those.

"And he's former NCIS, so he's used to government crap." Cam waved his hand in the air. "Business crap is about the same."

Hope shook her head and mumbled something about men acting like boys. "Tony is pursuing the Mark-as-bad-guy story, I take it."

"As far as Tony is concerned, the case is closed."

She never broke eye contact with Connor. "But you disagree."

"Definitely." Davis took the question. "We're going to rip his company apart, look at every piece of paper and check out whatever angle we can find."

"We think Tony is at the heart of it all," Joel said.

"Then he needs to pay." Her hand clenched his thigh. "How can I help?"

Davis laughed, this time full and open. "I like her."

"Apparently she can shoot a bow and arrow, too," Cam added.

Connor's eyebrow rose. "That's impressive."

They didn't know the half of it. She could guide them all and outhike them. They were in shape.

The job demanded them to be, but she had stamina that beat them all. Joel was man enough to admit that…and then there was the part where he found it more than a little sexy.

Cam spun his mug around on the table, letting the bottom clank as it turned. "And she managed to date Joel without killing him."

"Amazing." Davis shook his head as his voice filled with awe.

Talk about a mood killer. Joel stepped in to end the conversation before it got completely out of hand. Last thing he needed was this group rapid-firing questions at her about his love life. "That's enough."

"In case you're wondering, he dumped me." This time she moved her hand and put it on the table where everyone could see it.

Yeah, that was definitely enough of this conversation now. Joel knew they were one step from him losing all control over it. "Can we not have this discussion right now?"

Davis's mouth still hung open. "No way he dumped you."

"I didn't believe it either," Cam said.

Connor's expression suggested he thought Joel needed serious counseling. "Always thought you were smarter than that, Joel."

"I'm starting to wonder." Joel mumbled the response before he could think twice about it.

If Hope caught it, she let it slide because she was already off to another topic. "There's one more thing. The… What did you call them, riggings? There's no way any of the men on the trip set those up."

Davis eyed her up, the appreciation growing with each passing second. "That leaves a rogue angry person or—"

"Charlie." Joel dropped the one name that kept kicking around his head.

The man blended into the background and didn't cause trouble. He also knew the area and could have hooked up the riggings and set the whole thing up. The question was why.

"My dad vetted him. Except for some financial issues due to down business like almost everyone else these days, he was fine." When a slap of silence hit the room, she looked around at each of them. "What?"

And there was the answer to Joel's question. "Money."

Davis blew out a long breath. "His background is a place to start. We'll run through it all again."

The room erupted in action. Connor started shuffling papers and Davis reached for the laptop. Even Cam grabbed a file and started looking through notes. Except for Hope's shell-shocked expression,

Joel loved this part of the team operation. They

had a mission and a direction. From here they could spin it out, look over everything and run through scenarios.

"Look for recent payments." Connor handed Davis a paper with a list of items on it. "See if anyone is helping Charlie pay his bills."

Hope finally snapped out of it. Her expression morphed from blank to furious. Those cheeks turned pink and she clenched the mug with enough force to break it in her hands. "I trusted him. He was out there with a gun, right with us."

"Kind of makes you want to punch him, doesn't it?" Cam asked.

Joel reached over and took the cup out of her tight grip. "Stand in line."

Chapter Fourteen

Tony slammed his car door and walked to the designated meeting spot. He passed other cars in the parking area under the Whitehurst Freeway and kept going until he hit the gravel spot at the far end, away from the bulk of the foot traffic.

It was the middle of the afternoon and traffic whizzed by. Georgetown was a mass of tourists and students. People talked and screamed as they fought for coveted parking spaces and swarmed in a large swath from the waterfront to M Street, where most of the stores and restaurants sat.

Charlie had insisted they meet or he'd start spilling everything he knew. Tough talk for a man with all of the blood on his hands.

After taking the last few steps with his dress shoes clicking against the pavement, Tony stopped. This close to the water the fish smell hit hard, but Tony didn't plan to be there long.

Have his say, issue his threat and go.

Charlie leaned against the driver's side door of

his dark truck as he glanced around, looking at everything but Tony. The dismissal made Tony regret ever making a deal with this guy.

Tony didn't wait for small talk. After a quick look around to test for privacy, he jumped in. "We agreed not to contact each other right now."

Charlie dropped his cigarette on the ground and stomped it out with the heel of his hiking boot. "Yeah, well, a lot of our plans got mixed up."

"Which is why it's even more important you lie low and keep quiet." If he refused to do that, Tony would have to make a new plan, one that included taking Charlie out.

The man was older but still fit. One of those guys who could fall anywhere in a twenty-year age range and grizzled from all of his time outdoors.

The choice of Charlie made sense at the beginning. The man needed money and Tony needed a particular expertise. One of the tech guys mentioned his uncle in terms of providing an extra hand for moving storage data. Talked about the man being discreet and taking odd jobs. How he was a loner and very private.

Apparently the nephew should have added ruthless extortionist to the list. Charlie had information and thought holding it over Tony's head was the answer.

Never mind Tony was smart enough to cover

his tracks and divert the trail away from him. He even added in a bribery message from Charlie to suggest the old man made it all up for a big payday and Tony was nothing more than a victim.

He definitely covered his bases. Even now, he had a signal blocker and a gun with him for protection to keep Charlie from getting the jump on him. In a battle of his word versus the loner's, Tony would win. He made sure of that. No one would blame him for killing a crazy stalker if attacked.

Charlie crossed his arms and legs as he leaned back against the door. "You've been ignoring me."

"I'm letting the heat die down." That was only half a lie. The other had to do with moving the money out and burying a paper trail.

"Interesting comment in light of Perry's death."

"You didn't have to touch him." Tony shook his head. "Fire, what were you thinking?"

"It was a clever solution."

"It was sloppy and makes the Mark story we're trying to sell—"

"We're?"

"—harder to swallow."

Charlie just stared for a few seconds before saying anything. "Perry came along when I was moving Mark's body."

The man failed to do anything right. Charlie was told to stage a fall. They'd gone over the plan several times. No trouble. Moving bodies where anyone could stumble by was not in the instructions.

Tony tried to hold on to his patience and keep the advantage. "Why were you touching it?"

"You wanted an accident. I was trying to stage one." Charlie shrugged. "I looked up and saw Perry and had no choice but to hit him."

"Then you make it look like a joint accident. Like they went after each other or something. You don't leave the guy alive." Tony clamped his mouth shut as soon as the words were out. He was a businessman. A legitimate one. He didn't engage in this nonsense.

He'd pushed the guilt out. Mark and Perry were decent workers and deserved better. But the idea that his plans had gone this far off course was the one thing Tony couldn't take. Find the wife, get the job, make the money. Easy.

Baxter had seemed like the right place to make his mark. Until it wasn't and he had to reform it in the image he wanted. He had never expected the collateral damage, and that it kept growing to include Hope and Charlie just made Tony want out faster.

"That woman you picked caused that problem," Charlie pointed out. "She went looking for Mark. Practically jumped out of bed and went on the hunt the next morning. I had to think quick, and that meant hiding the bodies."

It all came down to Hope Algier. Tony thought putting his executives in a novice's hands would mean a smooth-running plan with an easy scape-goat. She wasn't watching and someone got hurt. It had happened to her before, so people would believe history repeated itself. She would be busy finding her way and getting used to the job while Charlie went to work.

The exact opposite had happened.

But that didn't explain everything. "Even so, you left Perry alive."

"That was a miscalculation."

Two men were dead and Charlie viewed it as a math error. Tony started to wonder if Charlie was more sociopath than loner.

Treading carefully was the only answer. Tony bit back the frustration whipping through him and did just that. "You need to back off."

"I want my money."

Tony waited until a group walked past. They were a good thirty feet away, but he wasn't taking chances, regardless of how low they spoke. "We can't move money around right now."

Charlie groaned as he pushed off from the truck and stood up. "We made promises to each other, Tony."

"And I will fulfill mine." Tony had perfected

the art of lying. Wearing a blank expression while delivering a sentence devoid of any bit of truth. All those years turning companies around, swearing he was there to help and then recommending a full-scale reduction in force, had hardened him, but the skills came in handy now.

"I'm in it for the cash."

"Go back to the camp—"

"You're not in charge here." Charlie slammed a hand on Tony's chest and kept him from walking away.

Tony stared down at the hand and dirty fingernails, then back to Charlie's face. Tony didn't aim for neutral this time. He wanted Charlie to know his disdain, to feel his hatred. "This is my plan."

"It stopped being your plan when you sent Hope Algier out there for me to handle."

When Tony saw a couple headed their way, he shoved Charlie's hand away from him. "She should have panicked, called for helped and all of this would have been fine."

"She's an expert with connected friends."

The other thorn. Between Hope, Joel and Connor, Tony had his hands full. He couldn't decide if the answer was to remove the problems or ignore them. Not feed the beast. Charlie didn't need to know about the conflict.

"I'll take care of the Corcoran Team." Tony

meant that as a vow. He didn't know how he'd do it, but he would.

"You keep saying that, but I don't see any evidence of you resolving anything."

They continued to talk at a near whisper as the couple turned and crossed the street. No one looked their way, but people walked by on the other side of the street. That was too close for Tony.

He pivoted until his back leaned against a freeway post and faced away from the street. "The timing is wrong."

"Not for me." Charlie reached into his open truck window.

The move had Tony shifting to inch his hand closer to his gun. "I have to settle my business issues first."

Charlie pulled out a new pack of cigarettes as his gaze slipped to Tony's hands, then to his suit jacket pocket. "I don't care about those."

"Listen—"

"No, you listen." Charlie tapped the end of the pack against Tony's tie. "You have one day to get my money. Then I take care of a loose end and leave."

"What loose end?" There had been enough death as far as Tony was concerned. They already had too many facts to cover and too much evidence to hide.

Then there was the bigger problem. Charlie had proved his lack of skills. Two times and Tony might be able to evade trouble. He could cover up and create backstories. A third was pushing their luck. If he moved into the spotlight one more time, Connor would never let this go.

"Hope Algier."

And touching her all but guaranteed trouble. Rafe would bury anyone who messed with his daughter. Charlie had already warned Tony that she was sleeping with Joel and the guy had a severe protective streak.

No, she had to be off limits. "She is too connected."

"She can die like anyone else."

"You don't understand." Tony leaned in and pitched his voice low. "This team, what you said about Joel and his relationship to this woman… you have to let this go."

"No."

Tony's back teeth slammed together as he stood up straight again. "Charlie, we've got to be smart about this."

"I agree. Get smart."

"What does that mean?"

Charlie unwrapped the cigarette pack and dropped the plastic enclosure on the ground. "Get my money and then get out of my way."

"I don't want Connor and his team on my tail."

Charlie opened the door to his truck. "Then do what you're told."

"Bingo." Joel leaned back in the leather conference room chair and rubbed the back of his neck.

"Want to clue the rest of us in?" Cam stopped just before taking a sip from a water bottle.

Joel glanced at Connor at the head of the table and Hope beside him. "Line of credit."

Hope smiled. "I love when you just say random words."

It only took a few hours and numerous calls by Connor to obtain information he shouldn't have been able to nail down. He excelled at convincing powerful and connected people to turn over personal information in the name of protection. In law enforcement, at utilities, it didn't matter.

Joel didn't know how, but Connor had the private numbers of officials and a direct line to government agencies. With Joel's tech help, the whole team had access to databases with firewalls no one should be able to breach. But they did.

As a result, financial documents, phone records, every credit card statement imaginable and even electric bills—seven years of Charlie's life—were spread out on the table in front of them. "Charlie had two mortgages on the camp, right?"

"Both of which are overdue." Connor leaned back in his chair. "There's no hope of salvaging the place absent a big payday. It's possible it hasn't happened yet."

"He also has another line of credit. One he carries at an astronomical rate. At first it looks like a credit card and I don't see any loan documents to support it, but he just paid it in full." Joel passed the document showing the paid-off line of credit to Hope, who read it before slipping it to Connor.

"He made the payment three weeks ago." She shifted the bank documents in front of her. "There's no record of money going through his bank accounts, personal or business."

"It had to come from somewhere," Cam said.

"I'll put Davis on this." Connor glanced at his watch. "He should be back at the office by now."

"He better be." Cam snorted. "He left hours ago."

Connor shot Cam a you've-got-to-be-kidding look. "I assume he stopped by to see Lara before heading to the office."

Joel understood the temptation. For almost a month after he left Hope, he'd still drive to her house, thinking to check in. The habit almost broke his will.

The one time he saw her coming home, he'd sat in his car for hours and waged a mental battle about whether to get up and knock on the door. After the need tore him apart he decided going in and out of her life was worse than leaving. But he'd blown that theory over the past few days.

"So how does any of this help?" Hope pointed to the almost negligible balance on the older man's business checking account. "He still can't keep the campground with this income. He can't charge enough to cover insurance and operating costs."

Cam scoffed. "Having two deaths out there isn't going to help business."

"Maybe we caught him at the beginning of a new career." Joel didn't know if he should be happy about that or not.

A shiver shook her. "Killing for hire? That's a horrible thought."

"Now we have a way to apply pressure." Joel slipped a hand under the table and linked his fingers through her cold ones. He tried to absorb the chill and the trembling.

Her other hand covered their linked ones. "If he killed Mark and Perry, don't we want to turn him over to the police?"

"We want Tony Prather to go down, too," Connor said in a soft voice.

"It makes sense he's involved. I'm not sure I'd bet my life on it yet, but it's more logical than Perry starting that fire." She made a grumbling noise. "I talked with Charlie several times and never suspected."

"Neither did we," Cam said.

Joel had to choke back the fury clogging his throat. He'd had the guy right there, right next to him out in the woods, and didn't pounce. He didn't know whether Perry could have been saved there at the end because he was in bad shape thanks to the injury and exposure, but Joel would have tried. It looked like Charlie had stolen that chance.

"We're paid to notice." But it was the *what could have happened* that had fury twisting in Joel's gut. "The bigger issue is how he put you in danger."

She tightened her hold on him. "Why would he want me dead?"

"I think you were a pawn." Connor delivered the news like he did everything else—straightforward and calm. "He underestimated you."

Cam clasped his hands behind his head as he chuckled. "I'm thinking people tend to do that."

Not Joel. He knew better. And he didn't find any of this funny. "Tony's going to pay for all of this."

"Again, you mean if he's involved," she said.

Joel had moved on to plotting the guy's take-down. "Uh-huh."

"Sounds like we have a plan." Connor picked up his cell. "Then let's get to work."

Chapter Fifteen

Exhaustion threatened to drop her by the time she got back to her town house that night. Her father insisted he see her before she headed home. Then his connection got delayed and they settled for looking at each other through a computer screen while he sat in an airport lounge somewhere. He ended the conversation by vowing to never travel halfway around the world and hours from an airport again.

She hadn't even found time to unpack from the campground. Her duffel bags and bow case, along with the arrows inside, sat on the floor right next to the front door. She needed to move them or she was sure to trip. If only she had the arm strength to lift more than a bottle of water at this point.

Before she could get from the foyer to the kitchen to get one, Joel wrapped his arms around her and pulled her body tight against his. "You okay?"

"A little shaky." Not that she needed to tell him. He must feel her shivering.

Ever since learning about Mark and seeing the evidence for murder pile up, her head had been spinning. So much danger and pain. The idea that money caused it all made her switch between wanting to double over and needing to hit something.

Not that she'd never experienced heartache or loss, but she'd been luckier than most in life when it came to the essentials. She got that. Her father had money and never withheld it or affection. She never worried about having food or shelter or being loved.

Joel missed all of those things and still she didn't know a better man. He didn't think the world owed him. He didn't try to gather all the "things" or believe only money mattered.

Now if she could just get him to understand loving her meant being there for her. Always.

He kissed the side of her neck. "You're tensing up."

"It's been a rough day."

"Hey." He turned her around until his lips hovered over hers and her body slid against his. "It's going to be okay. We'll get Tony and Charlie, if they're the ones behind this."

The poor guy thought the camp and all the horror there caused her reaction. It surely contributed to where her mind had gone. Confronted with so much death, she wanted to grab on to life and not let go.

But the sadness stealing over her came from him. From not knowing if there would ever be a "them" again.

She played with the second button from the top of his long-sleeve shirt, opening it and slipping it back through the small hole again. "We need to talk."

"No good conversation ever started that way." His smile faded as fast as it came. "Wait, you're serious?"

She couldn't be this close and hold her ground. She needed space for this conversation. Heck, she hadn't even planned to have this discussion now. But coming back and having all of her emotions back up on her drove her.

She pulled away and stepped back a few feet. "What are we doing?"

He frowned and his gaze traveled up and down her body, as if he couldn't understand what was happening. Maybe that was part of the problem.

"I think we should get some sleep." He paused after each word.

She recognized the tone. He knew something was coming and mentally prepared for the hit. Usually at this point, he shut down. He suggested sex or talked about needing a walk. Dodged and ran, his well-practiced M.O.

Suddenly she had to know the answer to the question that had plagued her from the moment he stepped off that helicopter—would this time be different?

Having him pull away wasn't a game she could keep playing. He left and she'd waited for him to come to her. Now he was here, likely because her father begged him or, worse, paid him.

"Joel, come on." She was surprised at the strength in her voice.

"Please don't do this." All the color left his face. "Not now."

"When then? Two months from now when you come back for the third time? Next year when you stroll back in for the fourth?" The words sliced through her. She could see the cycle repeated forever. Didn't even have to close her eyes to envision it because she's already lived through the first round.

He wiped a hand through his hair as he spun around and headed for the family room. He started to sit on the couch but stopped and paced instead.

His movements wild and his usual control fading, he turned to her. "Can't we just let this be it for now?"

The question pounded her. She didn't even know how her heart kept beating. "I don't even know what 'this' is."

His hands clenched at his sides. "I missed you."

The longing in his voice tugged at her, but she would not go to him. Too many times this argument ended with her giving in. Not this time. "I know."

"I love you."

"I know that, too." That was what made this so hard. He wasn't a jerk. He wasn't afraid to tell her what he felt. Maybe it would be easier not to know because being this close and not being able to push their relationship across the finish line destroyed her. "I love you, too."

"My life…" He closed his eyes right as a cloud of pain crossed his face. He dropped onto the couch with his elbows balanced on his knees. "I live with danger. Hell, I need danger."

"You protect people."

"You can phrase it however you want, but the bottom line is I thrive on the adrenaline. I'm not a sit-on-the-couch-for-days guy." He stared at the ceiling. "You know this."

"I know your past doesn't matter to me and your personality doesn't scare me." Not even a little.

She saw the man he was, all they could be together. If anything, knowing he survived such hardships, overcame so much, to become so decent and loving made him even more special.

His head dropped and went into his palms, but he stayed silent. Debating how to give comfort without getting sucked in, she slid in next to him and lowered his hand. A few seconds ticked by before he looked over at her.

"I know you're not your father." She brushed her lips over his hair. "You are nothing like him."

Joel trapped her hand between both of hers. "Yet."

"Ever."

He slipped his fingers through hers and held on tight. "I get antsy. Staying still makes me jumpy."

"Do you want to date other women?" She had to swallow several times to keep the ball of anxiety from racing up her throat.

"What?" He made a face as if he'd tasted something truly awful. "No, of course not. This isn't and has never been about needing other women. I only need you."

The wonderful things he said made the inevitable end so much more staggering. "Then explain it to me."

"It's like this wild thing inside me. I went to DIA, a job I thought I'd love, and got restless. I worked for your dad and left."

The lump in her throat refused to move. "You left me."

He lifted her hand and kissed the back. "I've hated every second without you."

The conversation kept spinning and she had no idea how to make it land. She went with the question that circled in her head. "Do you plan to leave Corcoran?"

"No." Fast and sure, he didn't even hesitate.

That wasn't a surprise to her. Watching his easy manner with Cam and Davis, seeing how Connor led, it all convinced her Joel had found a home with the team. He'd found friends. Even if he denied it, he'd found normal.

He might talk about being a loner or an outcast, but they accepted him and he didn't show any signs of bolting. Whatever it was that made him twitchy when he thought about a forever relationship with her was silenced when it came to work. A certain calm washed over him.

She was happy for him to have found a home of sorts, but jealous it wasn't with her. "Do you want to end this—whatever it is—with me so you can find something else? Maybe something better?"

"There's nothing better." He shifted, getting even closer to her. "You have to believe that."

She wanted to. "Oh, Joel."

"It's not a line."

"I know." She trailed the back of her fingers

over his cheek. "That's the point. You are with the one woman who understands you."

"It's not that easy."

She tried one last time to make him understand how evenly matched they were, despite their very different backgrounds. "I love having a home base but crave the outdoors. Life isn't about comforts for me. It's about nature and hiking."

"And climbing."

If she wanted him to face a demon, she needed to stare one down, too. "Yes, that."

"Will you try it again?"

Right now she'd say anything to get through to him, but she didn't want to lie. The deaths on the mountain that day had stayed with her. The ones at the campground probably would too. So much responsibility and so much failure.

With him she could get through it. He just had to jump first. "Will you stay with me?"

"Your need to be outside and the anxiety that gnaws at me are not the same thing. Your love is healthy. Mine grew out of a strange sickness handed down from my father."

"But you're a grown-up now."

"I get that."

"Then the only other explanation for your behavior, your decisions, is you're a coward." Not in life and at work, but he was when it came to her.

He dropped her hand. "Excuse me?"

He didn't move but she felt the chill as sure as if he'd doused her with ice water and walked away. To keep from grabbing him back or begging him to listen, she got up. The couch was too small and the room was too close.

In the past few minutes the walls had pressed in. This place, her sanctuary, fell over her like a cage.

She knew the word would prick at him. Strike at all he believed about himself. That's why she'd used it. He needed a wake-up call. If this was their last chance, and she was pretty sure from the ache around her heart it was, she intended to use every weapon to win the battle.

Her breath escaped in hard pants as she struggled to find the right words. "You have a woman standing in front of you who loves you. Loves all that you are and believes in who you've become."

He stood in front of her. "Hope, look—"

With a raised hand from her, he stopped talking. "We love each other. We certainly don't have any problems in the bedroom."

"Definitely not."

"Yet you push me away." The memory of every word, every excuse, hit with the force of a hard slap. "What can that be but cowardice?"

His jaw tightened. "Let's find a new word."

"I'd prefer if we found a new way to do this."

"Meaning?"

She took the final step and walked right off the emotional cliff. "You have to go."

"You mean for tonight?" His eyes narrowed as if he never dreamed she would draw the line.

She had to own that. Somehow, in some way, she gave him the impression he could always crawl back.

To be fair, that was their unspoken deal. She told him she'd be there while he figured out what he needed. He told her to move on. The final words hanging between them from last time strangled them now.

"If you can't get your act together, forever." She rubbed her hands over her bare arms, but her skin refused to warm up. "I can't do this. I can't love you and wait, which is exactly what I've been doing."

"Your father said you were dating." His chest rose and fell in hard breaths.

Tension snapped between them and choked most of the air out of the room. When she looked at him she saw a mix of anger and resignation in his dark eyes. His mouth stayed in a flat line and every muscle stilled.

She didn't know if the final warning or the idea of her with someone else put him in this place, but the loving man who wanted to go to sleep had disappeared. The hardened fighter remained.

"Those were fix-ups and dinners when I got tired of my father begging me to try." She wouldn't lie because that's not how she lived her life. This wasn't some silly game. "I don't know what he told you but I've barely kissed another man."

Joel's head shifted forward. "Barely?"

"I am here, Joel. I am yours forever. There is no one else and never will be if you reach out and take what I'm offering." Her fingernails dug into the skin on her arms as she threw down the final gauntlet. "But I'm done running after you."

He held out his hands. "What does that even mean?"

There was no way he couldn't know. She didn't engage in word games. "This time you have to come after me because I'm done being the only one trying to keep us together."

His hands dropped to his sides. "I never meant to hurt you."

"But you do. Every single time." Time after time, so many nights alone and desperate for him.

He winced.

She didn't back down.

Taking small steps, because that was all she could muster, she went to her front door. The knob felt heavy in her hand as she twisted. She would have thought she was trying to pull hundreds of pounds when she drew it open.

"Goodnight, Joel…and I'll hope it's not good-bye."

He didn't say a word as he walked past her into the dark night.

Chapter Sixteen

The next night, twenty-four hours after the love of his life had escorted him out of her house and his world exploded, Joel stood at the far end of a tree-lined road filled with mini-mansions and driveways loaded with expensive cars. They were tucked back in on a construction lot. The frame for a massive house loomed behind them, and a trash bin hid Connor's SUV.

In this neighborhood, parked cars and strange men walking around would be noticed. This was the kind of place where most houses had a live-in maid and the police on speed dial. No soliciting and certainly no gawkers.

They couldn't see Tony's house from this position, but it sat around the corner. As Joel would expect, Tony had bought the house at the end of the cul-de-sac on a double lot. From the pictures, with the white columns and three stories, the sprawling place looked big enough to be a school.

Joel grabbed his Kevlar vest out of the backseat of the truck. Concentrating on the straps and his weapon, he tried to push Hope's face out of his head. The pale cheeks and sunken eyes filled with pain.

He had done that. He had put her there.

He'd seen her cry exactly twice in all their time together. Both times he caught a glimpse as he walked out the door, never intending to return. Both times, the devastated look rammed into his gut until he moved his hand and checked for blood.

The first time nearly killed him. He feared this time would finish the job.

He tried to focus on the task in front of them— Tony. Finishing this off was the last thing Joel could do for her. Guarantee her safety.

Then he had to walk away. No checking up. No coming back. No answering her father's calls. Any contact resulted in wounds and the bleeding didn't stop.

"Tell me again about the intel." When neither Cam nor Connor answered, Joel glanced up. The concern was right there on their faces. He hated that, too. "Well?"

Cam held his gun in front of him, but instead of a weapons check, he stared. "You okay?"

More like smashed in little pieces. "I just want to run through the plan one more time."

Connor shut the driver's side door of the truck. "We've had eyes on the house."

Because there were exactly three of them in town, Joel didn't know what that meant. "Who?"

"Davis and Ben rigged something from back at headquarters using security cameras and I have no idea what else."

Joel did. He knew because he had created the program that snaked into private systems and everywhere else it shouldn't be. "Trade secrets."

Cam frowned. "What?"

"That's the name of my program. Ben's been helping me with the design and implementation." The guy's tech background proved helpful. He claimed to have limited knowledge, but combining their interests had created something with great promise in the field of surveillance.

"That's likely it then." Connor took out his cell and showed them a photo of the house one last time. With another swipe of his finger, he brought up the schematics and blueprints they'd all memorized, complete with a security system overlay. "Charlie came in about a half hour ago. The security system has been off since."

"He went in through the front door?" That struck Joel as something partners might do. Seemed they finally connected the dots on who had set the whole camp scene up and why.

"Only after making a lot of racket," Cam said.

Connor shook his head. "Tony might have had some concern he was coming because the wife left hours ago and hasn't been back. I'm guessing he sent her away."

Two men. A big house. Corcoran in control of the security system. Joel liked the odds and, because he hadn't liked a damn thing all day, it was a relief to stumble into some good news now. "What's the plan?"

Connor leaned against the truck's hood as his gaze toured Joel's face. Whatever Connor saw made him scowl. "What happened yesterday that has you snapping and stewing?"

No way could Joel handle this now. He doubted he could handle it a year from now. "Nothing."

Connor didn't let it go. "We need your head in this."

"It is." Joel vowed to close off his feelings and concentrate on the task at hand.

He knew all too well how to block his emotions. He'd call on those long-ago learned skills and drag them out now. Maybe they'd finally be good for something other than destroying his life.

Cam exhaled. "Hope—"

"Is not a topic I'm going to discuss." Shutting the conversation down, not mentioning her name, was the only way to get through this.

Cam and Connor exchanged glances, but Cam was the one to speak up. "I guess we have our answer."

With a click Connor set his gun down on the hood. "We can stand down and—"

"I want this guy. Both of them." This much he could do. Joel would not leave until the job was done. Then he could slink back to Annapolis and figure out how to regroup. "It's the only way I'll know she's safe."

"Then you'll leave her again." Cam's eyebrows lifted in question. "Right? That's what you're saying."

"Last time." Connor put a hand on Joel's shoulder. "Are you in a place to help us? Cam and I can go in and Davis can book it up here. At this time of night it won't take long to drive back from Annapolis. We can go back to the hotel and—"

"I'm fine."

Cam scoffed. "Yeah, you sound it."

"How about if I punch you? Will that prove it?" Yeah, knowing Cam's reputation Joel would regret it later. But blowing off some of the energy pinging around inside him would feel good at the moment.

"Go ahead. If that's what it takes for you to get your head out of—"

Connor held up a hand. "Okay."

"Are we going to talk or move?" Joel asked, hoping to get the conversation back on work and out of his private life.

Connor's eyes narrowed as he assessed Joel again. "We're heading in."

"Happy that's resolved," Davis's voice boomed over the mics they all wore. Tiny silver discs in their ears that kept them connected. They called it the comm. "For now."

Joel remembered the entire conversation and swore under his breath. "How long have you been on the line?"

"We all are—me, Pax and Ben—and as the three members with women, we'll talk to you about your idiocy later. Maybe let Cam knock some sense into you," Davis warned.

And they would. Joel planned to dodge that meeting. "Lucky me."

Connor picked up his gun. "Move out."

HOPE HAD GOTTEN as far as her couch. She thought about taking a shower. Dreamed about crawling into bed and not coming out for months. Instead, she slouched down on the couch and curled into a ball.

That's what you did when your world crashed down around you and scattered into a million unfixable shards. You cowered.

She curled tighter into a ball with her feet

tucked underneath her as she berated the choices she'd made tonight. This time she had no one to blame but herself. She could have played the whole scene better. Waited until morning, after they had gotten some sleep and some distance from all that had happened.

She could have doled her concerns out in short bursts to Joel instead of laying it all on the line. So many decisions and all of them seemed wrong in hindsight.

The goal was to force Joel to step out of the blackness that surrounded him and into reality. Talk about a miserable failure.

For someone who insisted she didn't play games, she certainly had done so tonight. She'd given him an ultimatum, something she vowed never to do again.

After so much death she thought he'd choose a life with her. At least fight back and insist they find a way, or that he have some time. But, no. He fell back on the old excuses and insecurities.

Her head dropped against the couch cushion and she snuggled in deeper. Her gaze fixed on a point above the fireplace. Not a photo or anything concrete. Just a spot.

She sat unmoving for what felt like hours. Her muscles ached and her head pounded from the crying. Her cheeks were dry now because she had nothing left. Not even the energy to get up.

Just as her eyes closed, she heard a gentle tap at the door. Her head shot up and she tried to remember if she'd set the alarm when Joel left…Joel.

The idea of seeing him, of him coming back, had her up and sprinting.

Somewhere at the back of her head, a bell clanged. All those lectures from her father about being careful. Joel's insistence that her place be outfitted with the best security system on the market. The warnings jumbled together as she hit the foyer.

The green light blinked on the alarm, meaning she'd typed in the code at some point and turned it off. She pressed a hand against the door and went up on tiptoes to peek out.

The wood caught her in the forehead. A slam and a crack followed by a blinding pain and spots floating in front of her eyes.

Her body reeled back and her socks slid on the polished hardwood floor. She threw out her arms to catch her balance, but the move only made her more tipsy. The room spun and darkness closed in at the edges of her vision. She had to shake her head to clear out the ringing.

When she heard the soft click, she looked up. Charlie stepped inside and closed the door behind him.

He smiled. "You need better locks, but thank you for making my job easier and turning off the fancy alarm. That I couldn't break. Well, not without some serious help."

His presence was so out of context. She didn't know what time it was or what was going on. "What are you doing here?"

He grabbed her arm and dug his fingers into her skin until she felt the bite and sting of his pinch and let out a soft gasp. She struggled to pull away, but he tightened his hold and started twisting.

"Good evening, Hope." He dragged her in closer until his breath brushed over her cheek. "You and I are going to have a little talk."

The rattling in her brain stopped long enough for her to blink out the cobwebs. "You're supposed to be back at the campsite helping the police."

"I'm done with law enforcement."

Of course he was. That's what happened with criminals and she had no doubt that's exactly what he was.

The truth washed over her. "You're Tony's partner in all of this."

"Was." Charlie smiled. "Now I'm your nightmare."

Chapter Seventeen

They entered Tony's house through the back gate as planned. Waiting to hear the distinctive click before going forward, Joel stood with his fingers wrapped around the handle. Once the noise came, he twisted and they slipped through the entrance usually reserved for gardeners.

Crouching, they jogged in the planned formation with Connor in the lead and Cam and Joel falling into a triangle behind him. Each one wore protective gear and blended in with the trees and darkness. Their shoes tapped against a patio as they moved by the building the plans referenced as a pool house.

Joel glanced up and locked on the motion sensor light by a hammock. When it failed to switch on, he knew Davis was working the controls from Annapolis like the expert he was. He heard what they heard and saw what they did through small cameras implanted in their helmets.

Joel often sat in that chair and orchestrated from

a distance. Even though it reduced the chance of taking a bullet, the task was much harder than it looked.

Lights shone along the whole back of the house. A wall of windows stretched across most of the bottom floor. Joel could see every stick of expensive furniture and a kitchen usually reserved for magazine spreads. He silently wondered if Tony ever ventured into it.

The one thing Joel didn't see was people, no one on any floor, though the top one stayed eerily dark.

Connor motioned for them to peel off and take their positions. He took the middle area and headed for the double doors off what looked like a dining room. Cam went left toward the garages and Joel took the right, aiming for a side door that led to something called a mud room. He assumed that meant a laundry or closet or something. Davis, who was knee-deep in renovating an old house, had tried to fill Joel in but he didn't listen to the particulars.

Pivoting around the outside furniture on the back patio and what looked like a heater, Joel hugged the hedge line. He skated away from the area just outside the doors, preferring the staggering darkness. Let Connor figure out how to stay unseen with spotlights hitting his head.

The darkness of night bothered others, but Joel

had trained to let his other senses run wild. Even now the smell of orange hit him, likely from flowers or a tree.

Slipping around the house took Joel out of the line of sight of the others. He could no longer see what they were doing or assess their progress. But because Davis hadn't reported a problem over the comm, Joel assumed there wasn't one.

The door was right where the plans said it would be. He reached up and turned the knob. It rattled in his hand but didn't budge. The sound bounced around the quiet night and Joel pressed his back against the wall, ready for an attack from any direction.

Wincing, he waited for a shrill alarm to sound. None came. He counted that as a win and let out the rough breath he was holding.

The rule was radio silence. That meant limited talking and almost no communication back to headquarters unless an emergency arose. Headquarters could talk all they wanted, right into your ear, but Davis was a pro. He knew that broke concentration and he stayed silent.

His breathing filled the line. Then a voice, no louder than the breath that came before, sounded over the line. "Open."

Joel reached up again and this time it turned. He held up the prearranged "go" signal in front of the helmet cam.

Keeping the opening as small as possible so as not to gain attention, he slid inside. The side of the door scraped his back but he ignored the slice.

Balancing on his haunches, he listened for any sound. This was a big house and the men could be anywhere. Good news was Davis reported only two people in the house, or such was the case a half hour ago when they did their check. They'd been watching ever since and no one else had come.

Music or talking would help guide him, but Joel didn't pick up anything. He heard the soft hum of the refrigerator and the usual creak now and then that all houses let out. Nothing that sounded like arguing or negotiating. Unfortunately. Looked like Tony was going to be unhelpful to the end.

Standing taller, Joel walked past the washers— two of them, because that seemed necessary for two people. He waited at the door and when he failed to pick up footsteps or any other sliver of movement or noise, he crossed into the next room.

This time he heard a sound. A thumping, loud and steady. It came from the area above his head. To sink through the floor and radiate through the house, it had to be pretty obvious upstairs.

Shifting around the long marble counter, he grabbed a small knife out of the collection in the block. Never hurt to have an extra weapon. The size, easy to tuck into the edge of his glove, gave him one more advantage. Or so he hoped.

In front of him loomed several doorways. He could see into a large room with a television. He closed his eyes and thought about the plans. He needed to go deeper into the house and find Tony's home office. If that didn't work, Joel would head for the stairwell.

But the thumping kept grabbing his attention. With a brief look around, he skipped the downstairs check and headed for the bottom of the stairs. Cam met him there. He pointed up and Joel knew they shared the same idea.

The double height of the entry let them study a wide area, but not every angle. The steps curved, so the top landing wasn't fully visible. Someone could be hiding, but Joel bet not.

Tony sat at a desk all day. He didn't plan attacks. The one he had tried to handle ended up with two men dead and too many questions. Joel doubted that went as hoped.

Careful to stay to the side and not to hit a creaky spot, they trailed each other up the stairs. Joel took the lead and kept his attention above them. The responsibility for scanning the area below and calling out about danger fell to Cam. Joel couldn't think of another man he trusted more with his back. Cam spent most of his time traveling, but they stayed in touch. The trip to the woods had only cemented their trust.

A huge chandelier hung over their heads, and the stair railing shone like it had been polished for days without stopping. There was one benefit to such an over-the-top house. Everything had a place. There wasn't any clutter and the plush carpet silenced their steps.

Nothing moved as they climbed, but the steady thumping grew louder as they reached the top. Though he tried, he couldn't place it. Not a weapon or any machine he recognized.

At the top, Joel stopped for a second to get his bearings. The master bedroom consisted of nearly a thousand square feet, more than the size of his last apartment, and sat to his right. He turned the corner and headed there. Cam followed right behind.

The door at the end of the hallway was open. Joel could make out something scattered all over the floor. Clothes, maybe. Papers, certainly. He knew there was a large sitting area in there in addition to the bedroom and bathroom.

He and Cam took positions on either side of the wide hall and stalked with their backs against the walls and their guns aimed in that doorway. Joel caught Cam's attention and glanced down at the floor. Cam looked, then shrugged. Whatever was going on in there stumped both of them.

The floorboard under Cam's feet creaked and the thumping cut off. That meant the end to their covert advance. One more step and the boom of gunfire started.

Both Joel and Cam dropped down. Joel crawled on his elbows, shooting as he went. Cam took the higher position but still kept low.

They pushed forward, emptying their magazines as they went. Bullets flew and artwork crashed off the walls. Something made of glass exploded near Joel's head and he ducked to avoid the shards.

Plaster from the walls kicked up and curtains bounced and shredded. Joel could hear crashing and shattering as their bullets slammed into all the furniture in the bedroom.

A mix of dust and smoke swirled around them. He sniffed for gas, because that seemed to be Charlie's specialty, but only smelled the sulfuric scent of gunfire.

A noise registered over all the banging. They stood just outside the doorway when Joel signaled for Cam to cease firing. It wasn't hard to make out the yelling now. Loud and male and near hysterical.

"No, stop!" The chant came from inside the room.

Joel didn't buy the surrender. He braced his body against the doorframe. "Come out."

"I can't." The thumping came in quick succession that time.

Cam asked what it was, but Joel didn't have a clue. "Why can't you walk out there?"

"I'm down."

Cam shook his head. Joel didn't believe it either, but a standoff in a shredded hallway wasn't his idea of a smart use of time. Not when they only heard one voice and there should be two.

"It's Tony Prather." Davis had voice recognition software on his side and a pretty good memory. If he said this was their guy, Joel believed him.

"Where's Charlie?"

"Gone."

A soft thud, almost hidden, sounded behind them. Cam spun around but dropped the weapon again when Connor's head popped up at the top of the stairwell.

"Who's in there?" he asked.

Joel repeated what he knew. "Tony."

Connor stepped around the worst of the debris, but small piles crunched under his feet. "I was in the office when I heard the shots."

"Help me." Tony's plea sounded softer and breathy that time.

Joel started inside but Connor held him back. "Tony, this is Connor Bowen. Where is Charlie?"

"He left." Tony's voice filled with panic. He groaned and something fell.

Connor looked to Joel, then Cam. "Believe him?"

"No," Cam shot back.

Connor nodded. "Let's go in and get him."

All three walked into the room with Connor in the lead. Broken furniture and clothes littered the floor. Papers and dust were everywhere. It looked as if someone had taken a wrecking ball to the place. Not a simple glass anything remained intact. Gunfire had shredded the comforter and curtains.

Joel recognized some of this as their work. But not all. Someone else needed to take credit for the opened drawers and the empty bag on the bed.

One thing was missing—Tony.

Filing in, they opened doors to massive closets and a room with boxes in it that Joel couldn't even identify. If it was a closet, it was a big one. To the right, Joel spied shoes. He snapped his fingers to get his teammates' attention. They all stopped and aimed.

"Come out, Tony," Connor said in a stern voice. "This is over."

"Can't." The guy practically cried now.

Joel recognized the tone as one of defeat and pain. He motioned them forward. The sight that greeted him would stay in his head for a long while. Tony slumped on the floor with blood soaking his shirt.

He balanced against the sink cabinet with his

legs in front of him and his hands limp at his sides. It looked like someone had taken a knife to him and enjoyed it too much.

Tony's head lolled to the side. Joel followed the line of his body to his foot. He jammed his heel against the door to another closet and it slammed against an inside wall.

A phone sat a few feet from his foot and just out of reach. Joel could only assume Tony was trying to reach it and kept moving his foot when the rest of his body failed him.

Connor squatted down in front of the seriously injured man and took his pulse. The guy's eyes were open but glassy. He was fading, and they had minutes only. Even then Joel doubted help could get there in time.

Connor glanced up at Cam. "Call for medical."

"Is anyone else here?" Joel thought about the report of his wife leaving and hoped they got that right.

Tony shook his head but didn't talk.

Cam talked low in the background and Connor went to work trying to stem the flow of blood from Tony's chest. Dropping to his knees, Joel took up the position on Tony's other side. He grabbed a towel off the counter and pressed it against the man's stomach. It stained with red almost immediately.

Tony's eyes closed on a hiccup of breath. Joel worried they'd lost him.

"Hope."

Joel leaned in. "What did you say?"

His heart clunked and Connor's hands froze.

Tony's head drifted farther to one side. "He wants her dead."

Joel grabbed the man's shirt in his fists to shake him awake again. This was about Hope and he didn't care what he had to do to hear the message. "This isn't the time for your bullshit."

Tony panted and his chest jumped up and down as he forced out words. "Charlie thinks she ruined everything."

Panic flooded through Joel as he sank back on his heels. He couldn't think. Couldn't breathe. He'd spent so much time walking danger away from her and here she was, alone with a nutcase on her tail.

"I'll call and warn her," Cam said.

Joel's entire world froze. He could hear Cam speaking and Davis saying something over the comm, but the sounds muffled and mixed until nothing made any sense. It was as if someone had fired a gun right next to his ear and taken out his hearing.

Joel looked at his boss. "Connor?"

"Take Cam." Connor held out his hand and

Cam dropped the phone in it. "I'll wait for the ambulance."

A question finally pushed into Joel's brain. "Did you reach Hope?"

Cam shook his head.

"He's going to kill her." Tony panted through the words but his eyes closed. His body became boneless as his hand fell open at his side. "I want him to fail."

HOPE FORCED HER mind to stop racing. She needed to stay calm. A madman stood in her home and her alarm system was off. Joel wouldn't be rushing in to help her. She didn't even know if he was still in town.

That left only a few options, the main one being to scream her head off.

Something flashed and a cold hardness pressed against her throat. A knife. "Don't try to be a hero, Hope. We've all had enough of that from you."

"I didn't—" She inhaled as the blade broke skin.

"One sound and I will cut you. Deep this time, whether I slice you or throw it at you. Do you understand?"

"What do you want with me?" Her voice wavered, but she had to keep him talking while she thought of a new plan. The front door was the best candidate.

"You ruined everything."

Charlie being here made no sense. He should be running. "I was just doing my job."

He shoved her against the couch and she fell deep into the cushions. Before she could bounce up again, he sat on the coffee table across from her. A second later he held her wrist in his grasp with the knife hovering right there.

He tapped the flat side against her skin. "Mark was supposed to disappear, but you had to go looking."

"Yes." She tried to pull away, but Charlie only tightened his hold.

"I told you Mark was blowing off steam and to let it go." Charlie shook his head and treated her to an annoying hum. "You never listen."

"But you killed him."

"That was the deal." He waved the knife in front of her face this time. Back and forth. "Pay off the mortgages and in return I helped Tony with a little problem."

"Mark was a human being, not a problem. And Perry. Was he just an afterthought?"

Charlie made a face as he stood up. "So many questions from the spoiled little rich girl, but I'm not going to play along. I'm not one of the men you have wrapped around your finger, like your daddy and Joel."

She watched Charlie move around her apartment, touching photographs and stopping at the front door to hit the lock button. The system chirped and the red light came on.

As if that would stop her if she had a clear shot to the outside. She would run and scream and he would have to track her down. She would go out fighting.

But she might be able to entice him with something he needed. "I have money."

"That's why this will look like a burglary turned rage-filled attack turned fire." He walked into the kitchen and grabbed a towel. "You die and I take some items and cash."

She bolted for the exit. He was on top of her before her hand hit the knob.

He smashed her into the door hard enough for it to shake on its hinges. Then he grabbed her around the waist and threw her. Her legs went out from under her. She put out her hands to stop her fall but landed in a sprawl on the foyer floor by his feet.

Her elbow hit the hardwood with a crack. Every part of her ached and her head throbbed. She didn't even remember it slamming into the floor, but it must have.

"That's enough of that." He crouched down in front of her. "Want to know what happens next, Hope, the expert hiker and climber?"

"Joel will be here any minute."

Charlie laughed at her. "I was outside and saw him go. He left you. Looked pretty happy to be gone, if you want to know the truth."

"That's not—"

"Ran to his car to get away from you instead of staying the night. What guy does that?"

She pushed that hurt out of her mind and concentrated on survival. Joel would want her to kick and bite and do whatever she had to do to survive. "He will come back."

"Not tonight. He's busy with Tony."

A new horror spilled over her. More bodies. More death. "What did you do?"

"My partner got greedy. Now he's dead." Charlie took the lighter out of his pocket and lit the kitchen towel. The fire swallowed one end in a second. "The trail leads to me returning to camp. Joel will go there, only to get the call there's been an accident."

Fear swelled inside her. She'd battled back flames at the campsite and it had taken all of her strength. Seeing even this small fire twisted her stomach in knots. "You didn't do so well with that before."

"This time it's foolproof. You die and the town house burns down." He stood up and threw the burning rag on the couch. The cushion lit with fire almost instantly. "I think Joel will get the message, don't you? He may have stopped one fire, but he'll be too late for this one. See, I made sure to be on the security cameras at Tony's house. I slipped out the side, but he'll think I'm still there, and in a house the size of Tony's without help, Joel will be there for a while."

The fire crackled and she heard a whoosh. She knew she had mere minutes. And Charlie would want her dead before the fire took hold and raced through her house. "You'll never get away with this."

"If I wanted to stick around, you're right. But see, I have the money Tony planned to hide and now I can leave. Let the banks have the campground. I don't care."

"Just go." The new attack made no sense. He was free. He could run.

"I've decided you need to be taught a lesson first." He stepped away from the fire.

She didn't hesitate. Crawling on her hands and knees, she headed for the bow case. She'd never get off a shot, but her arrows were clipped inside and the pointed end could cause some damage. The hard thumps rattled through her and jarred her from head to foot as she went.

Her hand had just hit the case when Charlie's foot appeared in front of her face. He stepped on her hand and she screamed.

"I warned you." He used a scolding voice.

It only emboldened her. Finding energy she

didn't know she had, she made a fist and punched the fleshy part right above his knee straight on and with all her might. It buckled and he doubled over, almost going down. The move took his weight off her hand and she made another lunge.

Smoke billowed around her and fire raced up the walls in long lines. She ignored it all and reached for the latch. She fumbled but got it open just as something stabbed into her hip. The sharp pain had her flinching, but she fought on.

Throwing the lid open, she ripped an arrow from the lid and spun around. Charlie crawled up next to her thigh with his knife raised. His chest shook from coughing, but all she saw was the madness in his eyes.

She had one shot and she took it. Gripping the arrow, she stabbed it right into his shoulder as hard as she could. He screamed and the knife fell to the floor. She thought about searching for it, but the thick smoke clouded her vision.

She looked up. The door loomed in the distance. She thought she'd fallen near it, but it wavered and blurred in front of her.

She tried to crawl, but her strength abandoned her and she crumpled to the floor.

Somewhere over her she heard a crack. The noise sounded familiar. She remembered it from the cabin and feared the ceiling was caving in.

Then a rush of warm air poured in and swept

over her. She heard her name. In her cloudy head, she thought the voice sounded like Joel's. She tried to call out, but her throat refused to work.

As the world went hazy, strong arms slipped under her. Fearing she'd slipped into a dream, she forced her eyes open and saw a line of flames headed her way.

But there was someone else in her dream. She lifted her hand, expecting to touch air.

Her fingertips hit warm skin. Reality punched through her.

Blinking, she forced her vision to settle and touched the face swimming in front of her. "Joel?"

"I'm right here, baby." His voice sounded harsh and faster than usual. But he sounded real, like he was actually there.

"It was Charlie." An illusion or not, he needed Joel to know. The desperation to get the words out broke free.

Then she was floating. Her feet had almost left the floor when a hand clamped over her ankle and tugged her back.

The jolt revived her. Joel held her. They were in danger.

She looked down the length of her body and saw Charlie's furious face. She turned to warn Joel about the knife, but she saw Joel's gun.

He tucked her head against his shirt and brought her body in close to his. The roar of the shot broke through the thunder of the fire. It boomed in her ears and she rushed to cover them.

After one sharp crack, all pressure was gone from her legs and Joel stumbled back. Freefalling, she tried to get a sense of where the flames were and realized they raged all around them.

She heard people talking and the wail of her alarm before she smelled fresh air. When her back hit the grass, she believed she'd finally slipped into that welcoming dream. Before she could settle in, the coughing started. She turned her head and hacked as the scent of fresh grass filled her head.

After a few minutes she lay back down. She tried to gulp in breaths of fresh air as the realization hit her—she was alive. Which meant…

Joel's face hovered in front of her. "You're going to be fine," he said.

She thought she heard Cam and a neighbor. Sirens screamed in the distance and all around her. None of it made sense. It was so dark and she'd lost track of time. "What's happening?"

"You're safe."

She saw it all now. She sat cradled in Joel's arms as people rushed around them and Cam repeated something to Joel, something she couldn't understand. For some reason she needed to tell him one more thing.

She grabbed on to Joel's shirt and tugged him closer. "I love you."

Then the world went black.

Chapter Eighteen

Joel would never forget that moment. The SUV had screeched to a halt in front of her place and the whole first floor was aglow with orange flames. He searched the crowd that had gathered, looking for her and shoving people aside without thinking.

When he didn't see her, he rushed to the door. Cam grabbed his arm and told him to calm down, but Joel was desperate. Filled with panic, he kicked and the door slammed open then the alarm went off.

The gun. The knife. The blood. It was all so much to take in.

The sound of her voice as she'd told him she loved him was playing in his head now. Even as he sat by her bedside at the hospital and the loud-speaker squawked, he remembered her final vow of love.

The smell of disinfectant slammed into him. At least the dragging numbness had worn off. He rubbed his thumb over the back of her hand

and stared at the crisp white sheet pulled up to her chest.

He'd come so close to losing her. If any one thing had gone wrong he would have lost her. The traffic had worked for them thanks to some stoplight maneuvering by Davis. Cam drove fast enough. The door gave on the first kick.

Knowing about Charlie's wound, Joel also knew she'd saved herself. That was his woman. Strong, confident and fierce. The only bad news was the guy would live.

Tony wasn't so lucky. Charlie had unleashed on his former partner, leaving him no chance for survival. Remembering the state he was in, Joel thought it was probably a miracle he had made it until they had found him.

Cam stuck his head in the doorway. "Is she awake?"

"Not yet." Joel took in Cam's ripped and bloody clothing and wondered why someone hadn't taken one look at him and called the police.

Of course, they were crawling around but Connor handled them, as always. Cam looked as if he'd been dragged by a truck. Joel guessed he looked even worse himself.

"Where's Connor," he asked.

"Still talking with Hope's dad."

Talk about taking one for the team. The older man had yelled at Joel via cell phone during the entire ambulance ride to the hospital. He promised revenge if Joel didn't get his act together and treat his baby girl better.

Joel didn't blame the guy. He'd done a pretty lousy job of protecting her. The one thing he excelled at was leaving, and tonight doing so had almost cost her life.

He didn't know what kind of husband he would be. Hell, he wasn't sure he even ranked that high on the boyfriend scale, but he wasn't letting her go. Not again. He'd had a glimpse of life without her and he'd rather be selfish and hold her tight.

"At least he's back in town," Joel said, remembering the worry in her dad's voice.

"He's not happy about any of this."

Joel looked at her still form and a new wave of anger crashed over him. "That makes two of us."

The nurse came in wearing an official badge and dragging a tray behind her. The only way for her to get by Connor just outside the door was to be pre-approved by Corcoran.

More than one doctor commented on the overabundance of caution. It was nothing compared to the contingent of police assigned to watch over Charlie one floor down.

The nurse nudged him away from Hope's side. "I need to check her bandages."

He held his ground. "I'll stay."

"You should step outside." The woman was

five-feet-nothing and she stared him down like she would take him out.

He thought about arguing until he saw the smile on Cam's face and conceded. "Fine."

Joel waited until they stepped into the hallway to tell Cam what he should have said hours ago. "Thank you."

He brushed a square of what looked like part of a curtain off his upper arm. It could have come from anywhere since they'd been fighting all night. "For what?"

"Everything." Joel didn't even know how to put his gratitude into words. "I know you were supposed to be on vacation."

"Fighting fires is more interesting." Cam clapped Joel on the shoulder and nodded. From Cam, that was a huge show of emotion. "Besides, I was going to fly anyway."

It was the way he said it that had Joel questioning. "Where?"

Cam glanced at their boss where he passed back and forth a few feet away in front of the nurse's station. "That was up to Connor. He asked me to take him to Jana."

Now, there was news. "What?"

"He stayed to help you instead."

"Because I recognize a man in love." Connor stepped up and stared Joel down. "Do you?"

The conversation left Joel speechless. Connor

back together with Jana, or trying to be. Davis and Lara. They gave him hope.

Cam groaned. "Don't do it, man."

Lost in his thoughts, Joel lost track of the conversation. "What?"

"Don't give a list of excuses why it won't work with Hope."

Before Joel could answer, Connor launched into a speech. "One thing you might want to remember is that not being with her in this case made her vulnerable."

"Okay, but—"

"I'm not saying that to make you feel guilty, because this wasn't your fault, but being away from her didn't make her safer." Connor wound down long enough to exhale. "You're not your dad."

"I know." For the first time, Joel believed it. Unlike his father, he fought for other people. He believed in people. He possessed a sense of humanity.

Hope had told him so many times. Having a woman like her love him should have clued him in. She wouldn't waste her time on a dangerous loser. He got it now.

"No, you don't, but if you give that woman a chance she'll show you." Connor's comment came out almost as an order. "Be half as smart as I think you are."

Cam nodded. "Or her father will kill you."

"It doesn't matter what he thinks." It really didn't. It was great to have his support and his blessing, though right now he was pretty displeased, but Joel didn't need her father's opinion. He had Hope and she believed in him, even when he didn't believe. That meant more than anything else.

"Joel, come on."

He held up his hands. It was either that or listen to these two try for the next two hours to convince him of something he already knew. "I'm saying that because I already know living without her isn't an option."

Cam threw up his hands. "There, was that so hard?"

"Actually, I think the hard part is ahead of him," Connor said.

Cam barked out a laugh. "I hope she makes you beg."

HOPE SLOWLY AWAKENED. She saw the white ceiling and heard the beep of machines. She closed her eyes and mouthed a little thank you. She wasn't dead.

A deep male laugh had her turning her head. One she recognized and savored whenever she heard it. Joel sat in the chair next to her bed looking all rumpled and scruffy and far too delicious.

When their eyes met, he stood up and came

to the side of the bed. Bending down, he slipped an arm over the top of her head. "No, you're not dead."

"You wouldn't let that happen."

"Never." His fingers danced across her skin. "But we should really thank your quick thinking."

That's not how she remembered it. "You pulled me out of the fire."

The memory played in her head. She'd thought it was some weird dream, but it wasn't. His strong hands and words of encouragement. The firm grip and the gunshot. Her ears still rang from that, and a high-pitched ringing sounded as if in the distance. She knew from experience on the shooting range that that would eventually go away.

His fingers slipped into her hair. "You saved yourself. I was just there for the ending."

The word cut through her. She closed her eyes to beat back the pain as a new series of memories hit. Him leaving and her crumpled in a ball on the couch.

"Hey." His thumb rubbed over her forehead. "It's okay. Charlie can't hurt you now."

He had the wrong nightmare, but she opened her eyes anyway. "Is he dead?"

"No."

In a way, the news was a relief. She wasn't responsible for killing the man, and this one would've been on her. No accident. She'd stabbed him and had meant to…and would do it again.

But the idea of him being out there and alive in society made her stomach twist. "Did you catch him?'

"Pretty easy to do after you hobbled him."

She smiled at that. "I'm not sorry."

"Me either. I just wish I'd been there a minute or two sooner."

She wished he'd never left. Now that the thought was in her head, she wouldn't think about anything else.

"Are you leaving?" The question burned her throat, but she forced it out.

Looking into those eyes, all soft and sweet as he stared at her, broke her resolve. She wanted to take back everything she'd said to him at the house and call him back to her on whatever terms he wanted. The expression was the very definition of love. She had no idea how this man could continue to bring so much pain.

"No."

The word clashed with her thoughts. "What?"

"I've walked out on you twice." He leaned down and placed a small kiss on her nose, then pressed one against her lips. "I'm so sorry I hurt you."

Tears pushed at the back of her eyes. She refused to let them fall.

"You break my heart." She had told him so

many times how much she loved him. This time she wanted him to understand how much pain he inflicted.

"Never again."

She tried to move her head, and the bed flipped around on her. Apparently she had a head injury. At some point she would have to take stock of all the bumps and bruises and figure out why her hip ached so much.

Then she'd deal with her town house and not having a place to live. Right now the combination of it all was too much to handle.

Especially when she was trying to grab hold of this conversation. "What are you saying?"

He snuggled in closer, careful not to jostle her or move the pillow. His face rested right above hers, and those dark eyes were as clear as she had ever seen them.

"My father wouldn't have put aside his own needs and tried to rescue you." Joel kissed her on the mouth, short and quick. "He wouldn't love a strong woman like you." This time the kiss lingered and heated. "He wouldn't work for a place like the Corcoran Team. I am not him, nor will I ever be."

Her heart jumped. It was as if she nodded off to sleep and woke up to him spouting the things she'd been telling him forever.

But he wasn't spitting the words back. He